MISSING,
PRESUMED
DEAD

By the same author

Accident By Design
Bring Forth Your Dead
Dead on Course
Death of a Nobody
For Sale – With Corpse
The Fox in the Forest
Murder at the Nineteenth
Stranglehold
Watermarked
Who Saw Him Die

MISSING, PRESUMED DEAD

JM Gregson

This first world edition published in Great Britain 1997 by
SEVERN HOUSE PUBLISHERS LTD of
9–15 High Street, Sutton, Surrey SM1 1DF
by arrangement with Breese Books Limited.
This title first published in the USA 1997 by
SEVERN HOUSE PUBLISHERS INC., of
595 Madison Avenue, New York, NY 10022.

British Library Cataloguing in Publication Data

Gregson, J. M. (James Michael)
        Missing, presumed dead.
        1.   Detective and mystery stories
        1. Title
        823.9'14 [F]

        ISBN 0-7278-5153-5

Typeset by Ann Buchan (Typesetters), Middlesex.
Printed and bound in Great Britain by
Hartnolls Ltd, Bodmin, Cornwall.

PROLOGUE

The body lay still beneath the water. Its wide, unblinking eyes stared upwards, towards the surface they could never see. This was quiet water, with little disturbance to its surface between the high, untrodden banks. A century and more ago, men had dug and blasted their way into the earth here, in search of the granite that had built the solid houses of the industrial towns. It had not been a large quarry, partly because the slabs of stone here were not extensive, partly because the red Accrington brick of the area had been more popular with the late Victorians.

The pool which had long since filled the quarry was scarcely twenty yards across but the depth was almost as great. A few bold boys had swum here until the land was enclosed for its present purpose in the twenties. Since then the surface had been scarcely disturbed. The sun climbed high above the dark pond in the summer but on many days its was the only face that looked down upon the unruffled surface.

Once the body had reached the bottom of the pond, it was not disturbed. The weights which held it had been securely attached; they held it motionless when it became bloated with air after a few days, anchoring it against any rise. For a little while, the corpse pulled gently against the restraint. Then a few bubbles rose unhurriedly and sporadically to the surface. If the curlews wheeling in the grey sky above saw the tiny ripples, they showed no reaction. And certainly there was no human eye to remark upon the movement of the water. This was a quiet, well-chosen place.

There were no fish in this high, land-locked pool. Dark weed flourished in the deeper centre of the pool, so that no one could have seen more than six of seven feet down into it, even when the light was at its summer best. With so little life in the pool to damage it and the temperature generally so low, the body lay intact for a long time, facing that cool surface many feet above it which it would never see.

It was deposited in the pool at the end of October. In this high place, there were no trees to pollute the waters with their November leaves. The still surface froze quickly with the December frosts and the ice remained for most of the next two months, when the tracks of hungry birds and the occasional small mammal were the only blemishes on the thin layer of bright, untarnished snow which was the body's last coverlet.

As the days became weeks and the weeks stretched slowly into months, the murderer kept calm. It was an effort at first, but it was surprising how quickly the early speculation died. A nine-days-wonder, that was the expression. And it was surprising how accurate it was; when there was no further development to follow up the disappearance, other and spicier items of news soon replaced it, even in the local press and on the local radio.

The police would have it on file, of course. But a missing person is merely one of thousands, dutifully recorded but not energetically pursued. Only a murder attracts the full intensity of police interest and resources. And there seemed no reason now why this disappearance should be transformed into anything as brutally exciting as that.

When winter became spring and spring passed into summer, the murderer relaxed. Killers are supposed to return to the scene of their crimes, as if drawn by some undefined compulsion. This one went several times and looked into the pool, when it was safe to do so. But that was merely to check that all was well, as it clearly was. The intervals between these visits became longer. Then, with a little effort of will, they were abandoned altogether.

When the months became years, the murderer began to feel safe.

CHAPTER ONE

Detective Inspector 'Percy' Peach was wishing he had never seen a golf course.

Cricket was a much more sensible game anyway and he had at least shown some competence at that. His short legs and nimble feet had danced down the pitch and chastened many a truculent bowler in his time. Then someone had persuaded him to try golf.

At golf, you approached a dead ball, in your own time, dispatching it when you were ready into what had always seemed a generous area of ground, when he watched it on television. It had to be a doddle, a game for overpaid wimps and women with too much time on their hands.

And yet you made a fool of yourself.

Well, Peach had got used to that, reluctantly, over the months of his apprenticeship to this infuriating business. On the public course to which he had been lured by his colleague, there had been widespread evidence of incompetence, some of it much greater than his own. And amidst much hard swearing, none had been more intense or inventive than his own. In that respect at least, he could hold his own in this stupid new sporting world.

He had got used to hacking his way round the public course, with mud up his trousers in the winter and balls bouncing off the hard-baked greens in summer. Life was a bugger (only effete southern poofs thought of it as a bitch) and for most of the time golf seemed to Percy Peach a microcosm of life. And just occasionally, as when his ball soared high against an azure sky, the game offered a gratification to the soul, an aesthetic titbit to gratify that sense of beauty which Peach had long since decided it was appropriate for a copper to subdue.

He never voiced any such mawkish idea, even to himself. But the idea must have got through to his companions. For they suggested he should join a golf club. They even put to him that most dangerous and unfair of propositions, that it might improve his game. Beguiled by this vision of a path to the Holy Golfing Grail, Percy had succumbed.

Indeed, Peach had not only succumbed, but gone wildly over the top. He had applied for membership of the North Lancashire Golf Club. This was not only a private golf club, but the most exclusive one in the area. It would have been enough to set his old dad spinning in his grave, thought Percy. The old man's only sporting hero had been Tom Finney and he had thought golf courses the playgrounds of the plutocratic parasites who lived off the backs of the workers.

It was his mother who had insisted on the forenames of Denis Charles Scott for him, in recognition of the teenage idol she had queued outside Old Trafford to watch in 1947, though even the old man had admitted under pressure that that effete southern Brylcreem Boy Denis Compton could bat a bit. And when the twinkling feet of the young Percy had danced down the wicket in the northern leagues, his dad had come to watch, had even shyly revealed to the spectators beside him, 'He's my lad, is yon!' But he would never have countenanced golf. It was just as well perhaps that Mum had had the old man cremated.

He had been told when he put in his application for membership that he could forget about it for a year or two. But surprisingly soon, he had been called for interview. Perhaps it had something to do with the young sergeant who had proposed him, who had a handicap of three and had been a member of the club since he was a boy. Perhaps it was the general desire of golf clubs to have friends in authority; many organizations still hold to a pious hope that a detective inspector within the ranks is some sort of insurance against trouble with the law.

Whatever the reason, Percy Peach now found himself pitchforked much earlier than he had expected into this evening's embarrassing ritual. People who applied for membership of the 'North Lancs' were interviewed first by two members of the committee, that all-powerful male junta of the golf club. They had asked the expected questions, and Percy Peach, veteran of many a promotion board, had given them the expected answers.

But then there was this. A cocktail party, to enable all members of the committee to meet the latest group of candidates for membership. 'To enjoy a pleasant social exchange over a drink with them,' the letter to the victims had said. And then to meet in private afterwards, to decide the fate of their applications for membership. To blackball them, if they chose, without redress, without appeal, however mistaken their decisions might be. No one pretended the system was fair, still less democratic. But if you didn't like it, you could take your application elsewhere. This was a private institution, which could set its own rules. The North Lancs Golf Club made that defiantly clear.

Percy Peach decided as the evening proceeded that he did not like this system. That he wished he had never applied. That he hated the hypocrisy of being assessed whilst he was supposed to be in a friendly social exchange. Percy had never been much good at friendly social exchanges.

But he was here now, and stuck with it. He held the gin and tonic he had thought the diplomatic drink at the end of an arm crooked carefully at forty-five degrees, kept an increasingly glassy smile afloat, and listened. And whilst he listened, he sweated. His professional talent was to make others talk, and others sweat; he was not used to this, and he did not like it.

Part of his problem was that he had little experience of

the casual and friendly chit-chat which was supposed to be the basis of this exercise. As far as Percy was concerned, you asked questions when you wanted information. You offered opinions when they were asked for, or when you wanted to express some strong emotion. About queers, or judges, or women who lived off their ex-husbands. This gathering did not seem the right setting for his trenchant views on such things.

'You'll be welcome new blood in the club. If we accept you, that is. But I expect we shall. We're looking to lower the age profile, you see.' The florid moustachioed face in front of him barked these thoughts but added a yellow-toothed grin to signify they were friendly ones.

It was some time since Peach had thought of himself as young blood. He was thirty-six but for a policeman that was middle-aged. In any case, he looked older, with his baldness; Percy was used to playing the reactionary old sweat among his colleagues. Looking round the golf club lounge, he realized that he was one of the youngest people in the room. 'I'll try to behave well,' he said with a nervous giggle.

There were a hundred petty criminals in the area whose flesh would have crept at the horrid sound of a Peach giggle. This man seemed to take him perfectly seriously. The florid face nodded. 'Standards are all to pot, everywhere. Caught a fellow trying to come in here without a tie last night.' The watery eyes looked Percy up and down, until the detective inspector felt as though he were back in short trousers with his socks askew. 'You're a bit bloody short for a policeman!' the mouth below the grey moustache said accusingly.

'Yes. Well, the height regulations have been relaxed a little, you see. And I suppose in CID work it's – '

'All big buggers in my day, they were. Slapped you round the ear if you answered back. Bloody good thing. Taught you about life.' Percy thought he detected a seam of reaction here which he might usefully mine, but the face said with what was almost a snarl, 'Well, can't let you monopolize me, young feller. Must get on and give the other poor buggers a chance, you see.' Peach found himself staring at a broad dandruffed back, trying not to apologize for trespassing upon the old man's time.

Before he could recover, a voice trilled, 'Ah, another promising recruit for our social functions.' This was an accusation that Peach had never met before in his eventful life. He had never been an asset to any social function, as far as he was aware. He was rather proud of that.

He struggled to answer the lady's suggestion with the precision it seemed to demand. 'Er . . . um . . . What? Oh, I don't think – you know . . .'

'Don't be modest now. I bet you're capable of some nifty footwork on the dance floor!'

Percy didn't know the answer to that. The last time he had shown nifty footwork on the dance floor had been in pursuit of an arrest. Three arrests actually, and successfully achieved. He could remember the satisfaction of frog-marching the thugs to the car with their arms up their backs. But this hardly seemed the moment or the audience for graphic recollections of Toothmug Johnson and Poface Munro.

He peered at the tag attached to the mohair in front of him, hoping that it did not look as if he was assessing the rounding of the breast behind it. It told him that he was speaking to the Ladies' Captain of the North Lancs. She was shorter than him, so that even from the height which florid-face had just found so suspect he could look down into the humorous brown eyes. These were assessing him with a disconcerting amusement. The face had small, well-formed features, of which the most obvious was a nose which turned minimally upwards at the tip. The figure beneath the face was trim but certainly not straight.

It was another blow to his expectations on this disturbing evening. Golfing females who attained the office of captain were supposed to be ageing Amazons, without discernible waists or senses of humour. This one could only be in her early forties and he doubted if she weighed more than eight stones. 'Christine Turner,' she said, holding out a slim white hand. 'I tried "Tina" for a few years, but then that inconsiderate pop star came along and my children made me change.'

Peach made a despairing attempt at insouciance. 'I've only really thought about playing golf. But I expect I shall use the clubhouse facilities, when I get to know a few people. They're' – he looked round desperately – 'they're very nice, aren't they?'

She grinned at him: he had a disconcerting perception that she was reading most of his thoughts. If so, she was finding them amusing. 'Quite posh, aren't they? In a suitably bourgeois sort of way.' That was an adjective he didn't associate with golf club women. 'Does your wife play?'

'No. She's . . . well, she's – '

'No longer around?' It was true then: she could follow his mind. Peach, who spent most of his day convincing criminals that he followed their every squalid thought, squirmed his toes beneath their shining black leather. She said, 'It's becoming the rule rather than the exception, isn't it? Have you a current companion?'

'No. I – well, the job doesn't really lend itself to long-term relationships.' He was fleetingly proud of that phrase: those damned social workers had given him something at last.

'I can see you'll be a danger to all our ladies who haven't got long-term relationships, Mr Peach.' She threw his phrase back at him, the corners of her neat mouth crinkling upwards.

Before he could decide how to refute this outrageous suggestion, she was gone, moving on resolutely to surprise the next unthinking applicant who had brought his preconceptions to the club with him.

He was left with the secretary of the North Lancs, Paul Capstick. He talked of the petty pilfering which had beset the club and its car park, with the obvious implication that the admission of a detective inspector to the membership would eliminate such problems overnight. Percy was on more familiar ground here. He thought it diplomatic not to deprecate the suggestion completely, as it seemed it might help his sinking chances of membership.

Peach left it to the secretary and another committee member, who was drawn as if by a magnet to the discussion, to lead the way over the virtues of birching and a revival of National Service. Then he pointed out modestly that you had to catch the buggers first, and laid the first foundations of a reputation as a realist with wit.

It was only the last man he spoke to, an anxious-looking stooped figure whose label proclaimed that he was chairman of the Greens Committee, who mentioned his handicap. Percy had to confess that it was a modest eighteen, though he was 'hoping to improve with regular play on an excellent course.' That was a phrase he had rehearsed carefully before he came; he was rather proud of its mixture of sturdy confidence and unashamed creeping. This was a compound that had stood him in good stead at more formal interviews with his superiors in the police force.

He delivered the sentiment with all the aplomb he could muster but it still seemed to drop with the hollowness of its preparation into one of those sudden silences which fall unaccountably upon a crowded room. He did not like the collective smile with which the committee members greeted it as their heads turned towards him. They had the air of men who had heard such falsities many times before.

Percy Peach drove away from the golf club with the taste of crisps and gin and tonic like ashes in his mouth. He had not made a good impression, he decided. Not on those bigwigs in their golfing citadel; and still less upon himself. He was surprised how hard it had been to dissimulate, and how rusty he had become at the business. He was used to being himself, warts and all. With the criminals who were his means of life, he had even become accustomed to playing up the warts. Disguising them had not come naturally tonight.

He decided that he wouldn't be all that disappointed when his application was rejected by the North Lancs. Bunch of out-of-touch wankers, he declared robustly to himself.

He felt more at home as he approached the rougher streets of the older part of the cotton town. On other nights, he would have driven swiftly past the police car at the kerb and the raucous crowd outside the pub. Tonight he stopped and climbed out of his car. It was an assertion of a certain sort of integrity, though Percy Peach would never have recognized it as that.

The flying figure, looking back fearfully over its shoulder, came most opportunely out of the night, as if rewarding his decision. Peach's small but expertly applied foot caught the youth's instep with a wholly satisfactory precision. The man's momentum made him a projectile; he hurtled through the darkness and landed on his chest in the gutter eight feet away with an expulsion of air that rent the night asunder.

Percy had his foot between the narrow shoulder blades within a second but it was hardly necessary. The body was without air, its arms flung out above the head as if in supplication. After a moment, there was a shuddering in-take of air into the battered lungs; it shook the whole frame into a groaning life. Percy voiced the familiar words with unmitigated satisfaction. 'You're nicked, sunshine!'

He held the wrist gently until the youth struggled appre-hensively to his feet, then moved it firmly into the small of the slim back. There were grazes on the cheek and forehead, trickles of blood from nostril and chin, but apparently no serious damage. As the man made as if to lean on Peach's car, the DI moved the arm a little further up his back, squeezing out a little yelp of pain as the body straightened. 'Don't worry lad, you've still got two of everything,' Peach said. He pushed him five yards farther down the road, bent him almost on to all fours as he retrieved the knife from the spot where it had come to rest beneath the wheel of a van.

'Just fancy that!' said Percy, as he examined the weapon beneath the street lamp. 'Naughty lad, aren't you?' He pronounced the formal words of arrest as two uniformed men appeared panting from the darkness. 'This what you want, lads?' Percy Peach was back on familiar territory. Relief surged with the adrenalin through his veins.

Back in the North Lancashire Golf Club, Peach's golfing future was being decided. Only the committee would vote but, as a gesture towards democracy, all the people who had been at the cocktail party were invited to contribute their opinions before the formal session began. Even the one female who had been present was asked for her views: no one could say that the North Lancashire was not among the most progressive of golf clubs. It emerged that the Lady Captain had found Detective Inspector Denis Charles Scott Peach 'a likeable man beneath his natural shyness'. She thought it quaint but appealing that he liked to be called Percy.

Despite the handicap of this feminine approval, the committee subsequently found little fault with Peach's candidature. The red-faced chairman of the Development Committee even ventured the positive view that he might be 'the type of young feller we're looking for'. It was rare approval from this quarter and the younger men around the table had not the temerity to question the basis for the thought.

When the name was put to the vote and the bag passed around the table, no fatal black ball was slipped into its anonymous folds. While Percy Peach was consigning his captive to the cells, he was quietly accepted into the hallowed company of the North Lancashire Golf Club.

In the weeks to come, he was to wonder increasingly why he had ever applied.

CHAPTER TWO

Shirley Minton had finished cleaning the house. It didn't take her long, now that there were just the two of them. She often wished that there was more of a mess, as there used to be in the old days with the children around. The state they used to let their bedrooms get into! She smiled at the recollection, and her gaze switched automatically to the open door and the staircase she could see across the hall.

Well, there was no use living in the past: Derek was right about that. It wasn't fair to him, for one thing, and he was a good man. He understood what she felt about Debbie, as much as any man would. That was it, really: he was only a man, and you had to remember that. She pushed the vacuum away into its cupboard and got out a brilliant yellow duster. She had always liked a bright clean duster and she found that nowadays she looked forward to the tiny surge of pleasure it gave to her each day.

For she had to admit that she now dusted on most days. Once it had been once a week. Then, in the first days after Debbie had gone and she had been waiting for her to come home, it had become twice a week; now, as the months passed and there was no news from her, she had begun to go round the surfaces in the living room every day. She did not know quite when that habit had spread out to include the rest of the house.

It wouldn't be so bad, she thought, if she saw Charlie more often, even if a son could never be quite the same as a daughter. But Sussex was a long way away and now that he had the two young children, it wasn't easy for him to travel up to Lancashire. She understood all that. It wasn't just because he had never quite taken to Derek.

The two of them had got over that and it hadn't been too awkward when her son had come up for those two days at Christmas. She couldn't remember much about it now, except that she had felt Debbie's absence even more keenly when her son was with her. They had all tried to make her forget and be jolly but it was only natural that she should be sad, wasn't it? Someone had to keep the poor girl's memory green, after all. You needn't worry about that, Debbie love, whilst Mummy's here.

But come back quickly, love, won't you? Come back. Soon.

She moved round the room in the routine which had become so familiar that she had ceased to notice it. Even the moments when she paused to look out over the neat suburban back garden stretched to the same length each time now, though it was others and not she who had remarked on it. She wished sometimes that she could interest herself in the garden, as Derek and the doctor had tried to encourage her to do, but she did not like going out of the house much lately, even into the garden.

People saw you if you were out. And if they saw you they asked questions. She hadn't the patience for them any longer. It was all right people offering sympathy but of course they didn't really understand. You couldn't expect them to, she supposed, since they hadn't been through it. Perhaps when Debbie came back it would all be clearer to them.

She worked her way methodically round the room to finish at the sideboard, postponing until the last as usual the pleasure of the photographs. There were three of Debbie but she didn't spend long now on the ones of her as a child. She dusted the biggest one last, then held it in both hands to stare fondly into the shining face, with its broad mouth and perfect teeth. Last of all, she looked into the eyes, those wide brown ovals of perfect life, and found them laughing with her as always. Each day she had the secret fear that the smile would not be there in them, but each day that secret, intimate laughter which bonded the two of them together, was there for her to hear. She bent her head to kiss the picture. The glass was cold against her lips. Cold as the grave, her mother used to say. Well, she wasn't having that, whatever they all tried to tell her.

'You shouldn't be doing that, you know.' She jumped as if she had been stabbed. Her duster flew into the air and dropped soundlessly to the spotless carpet. But he had watched her silently for almost a minute, waiting for her to put the photograph down, so that she would not break the frame when she was startled. He went across and put his arm round her shoulders, feeling them trembling still with the shock through her cardigan, frightening himself with the strength of the love which surged through him at the feel of her suffering.

She said, 'I'm glad we had that taken, Derek, when she was eighteen. Coming into her majority, she called it. The little madam! You remember that I said it should be twenty-one?'

How could he forget it, when she mentioned it each time she touched the picture with him around? But he knew that it was just an excuse to talk about the daughter who had vanished. He took a deep breath, trying desperately to pitch in with a tone of optimism, not resignation. 'Shirley, I thought we'd agreed on something, old girl. You promised you'd look to the future, not the past.'

That again, she thought. Why can't they all leave me at peace with the little I have? She said, 'What future? I'm living in suspended animation; you should know that, Derek.' It was the phrase the doctor at the hospital had used. She didn't say he had told her she must get out of it herself.

Indeed, Derek Minton did know it. He thought of the one-sided conversations over meals. Of his arrivals home to find her staring sightlessly at the walls. Of the lovemaking which was without love, as one-sided as their conversations. Many times now, he would have welcomed a little open hostility. Those little, normal marital spats, with raised voices over the disagreement and laughing reconciliations in due course, seemed now to belong to a different world. He said hopelessly, 'You've got to face it, Shirley. Debbie may never come back.'

'She'll come. You'll see.' Shirley was still an attractive woman of forty-five, despite all this. But her seraphic smile made him understand how people who looked after geriatric relatives were sometimes driven to savage assaults on their loved ones as their resolute determination to live in a different world finally became too much for the carers.

She nodded now, looking out over the garden where the child had played before she grew into a woman, and he knew the exchange was going to be hopeless, even as he said, 'You have to face the fact that Debbie may never come back, love. Something – something might have happened to her. It's nearly two years now, you know. She wasn't the kind of girl who wouldn't get in touch, not in all that time.' He tightened his arm across her shoulder blades, wondering if the thought was too brutal for her, but as usual he need not have worried.

She shook her head, still with that childish, undisturbed smile. She did not even trouble to contradict him. She knew so much more than he did about her daughter, and that was an end of it, really. She wanted for a moment to say, 'You can't really know, Derek; you're not her real father, even though you were good to her and she liked you, even though she was happy to take your name.' But that would have been unkind, and she had no wish to hurt Derek, who loved her, she supposed, though she didn't think about that much, nowadays.

She looked back at the sideboard, at the pictures of her daughter as a small child, and felt a deep compassion for Derek because he had not seen Debbie in those carefree years, when he might have thrown her laughing above his head, as fathers did with young children, and caught the delicious infection of her laughter. What a giggler she had been, in those days! And how clever and how charming in getting her own way! Shirley said, 'Perhaps she'll come home, when the two years are up. She was always one for birthdays and anniversaries.' A little frown furrowed her brow for a moment. 'I'm still surprised she didn't come for her twenty-first, really.'

Derek Minton fought the despair which he felt dropping upon him like a dark blanket. Debbie's twenty-first had been an awful day, with the cake standing on the table and Shirley gazing down the road for the girl who all but she knew would not come home for the party. He roused himself to frame a last argument, 'That's just it, love. If she'd been going to come, she'd surely have come then. For her twenty-first. It would have meant a lot to Debbie to be here then.'

Somehow, without either of them noticing her stoop to retrieve it, the bright yellow duster was back in Shirley's hands. She had been twisting it gently between her fingers for a minute at least. Without looking down, fingering her way over the object as securely as a blind woman, she began to dust again the frame of her daughter's last picture.

The new Brunton police headquarters building was like any other office block. There were discreet notices near the entrance which proclaimed its function, no bigger than those which announced the insurance company in the next block or the northern branch of the electrical giant on the other side.

There were cells aplenty in the basement at the rear of the block and the interview rooms were suitably airless and austere, but the public saw none of these things, unless they got themselves into trouble. Only the vast size of the building proclaimed that crime was the great growth industry of the nation: the block had seven times as many rooms as the solid Victorian cop-shop it had replaced.

Percy Peach would have liked a more aggressive police presence – let the buggers know you're around and watching was his policy – but the architect had not consulted Percy. According to those who worked within this tower of computer Babel, he had not consulted any policeman. Otherwise he would not have put in a car park which was too small at the bottom and a huge oak-panelled conference room which was used on average once a week at the top. But the men and women who actually work in such buildings take too narrow a view, of course.

These thoughts passed in quick succession through Peach's mind before it switched to more trenchant ones about the people within the building. And in particular Chief Superintendent John D Tucker, Head of the CID section. Tommy Bloody Tucker, as Percy had grown used to calling him, had sent for Peach bright and early on this Tuesday morning. Before he was actually in the building, in fact. Percy had found the note requesting his attendance among the other papers on his desk. It had improved neither his morning nor his temper.

He pressed the button outside Tommy Bloody Tucker's office. The column of round lights to the right of the door said in quick succession 'Engaged', 'Wait' and 'Come In', then repeated the process in a more random order. It was rather like an inferior disco; Percy reflected that it had taken Tucker five years to master the command 'Come!' when people knocked at his door in the old building: he was never going to come to terms with this electronic wizardry before his eagerly awaited retirement.

Peach opened the door abruptly and discovered his chief still frowning over the buttons. He looked at Percy over the top of his glasses, then smiled in recognition. A bad sign, usually: he was not given to smiling at Percy unless he had bad news for him. It might be no more than a change in the duty roster, or it might be something much worse; it was just not possible for anyone to fine-tune the monitoring of the chief's facial expressions. Percy said, 'You wanted to see me, sir?'

Tucker's face clouded for a moment in the face of the challenge, then cleared. 'Indeed I did, Percy. Do sit down.' He waved expansively at the big leather armchair which had come with the room. These are bad signs, thought Percy, both the use of the first name and the request to be seated. Usually Tucker was uncomfortable enough with Peach to want him in and out as quickly as possible.

Tucker waited for a moment, studying the detective inspector's dapper grey suit and watchful morning face, waiting for curiosity to cloud the squat features beneath the fringe of jet-black hair. Peach remained stubbornly inscrutable, his pate shining as brightly white as his shoes shone black at the other end of his stock frame. Tucker was nettled into a little diversion. 'You weren't in when I sent for you earlier.' It sounded petty, even to his own insensitive ears.

Peach hastened to underline it as that. 'No, sir. I didn't hurry in this morning, because I was in here at almost midnight last night. Charged a lad with GBH and possession of an offensive weapon.'

Tucker's eyes widened. 'I thought you were off duty last night.'

Peach smiled delightedly. There was a use for Tommy Tucker after all. As a straight man. Percy said modestly, 'Oh I was, sir. But a good policeman is never off duty. I think I've heard you say that yourself, sir. When bolstering morale among the younger officers, I think.'

Tucker searched Peach's bland features for a hint of the insolence he thought he detected in the tone. 'Yes. Well, er, well done, anyway. First-class job. Got him banged to rights, I gather.'

'I understand he intends to plead guilty, sir, yes. Get him for causing an affray as well, I expect.'

Tucker looked down at the papers on his desk, striving for the casual note for his next inquiry. 'I thought you were going for an interview at the golf club last night, Percy?' He tacked on the first name like a man addressing a dangerous dog.

'The North Lancs, yes.' Peach dropped in the prestigious name with all the casualness which his chief had aimed at and missed. How had this bugger found out about that, he wondered. Was it the masonic grapevine? If it could land a wanker like Tucker in a job like this, it could certainly glean information easily enough. Percy tended to blame the masons for everything since he had found out that Tommy Bloody Tucker was one.

'Successful was it? The interview.'

Peach tried to look as if he was considering the matter for the first time. 'Oh, I think so, sir. Of course, I had the formal interview some time ago. I gather last night's exercise was just a social occasion – to let me see the club and meet a few of the bigwigs, you know. But of course, you'd know far more about these things than I would, sir.' He enjoyed that. Tucker was a member of the more mundane Brunton Golf Club and by all accounts far too much of a golfing rabbit to be proposed for the North Lancs.

Tucker said, 'Yes. Well, that isn't what I asked you to come in here to talk about.' He made it sound as if it was Peach, not he, who had raised the diversion of golf clubs; Percy bent his head apologetically, pleased that his shaft had so clearly struck home. He hoped more desperately than ever before that the North Lancs would indeed accept him.

The chief superintendent riffled through the papers on his desk, then said abruptly, 'We're going to lose DS Collins, you know.'

'No, I didn't know that, sir.'

'Well, we are. Partly owing to your report on his assessment form, no doubt.' Tucker made it into a peevish accusation. He hated disturbance, would have preferred that even the most efficient officers were held at their present ranks for ever if it kept his team intact and prevented his incompetence being discovered by new personnel. 'Collins is being promoted to inspector.'

'He deserves it, sir. He's a good man.' Peach would never have let Sid Collins hear him say that. He realized almost for the first time what an effective team they had been over the last three years: he as bouncy and aggressive as a bantam cock, Collins taciturn and observant, looking for areas where the soft touch might complement his inspector's belligerence. They were physical contrasts, too; the station referred to them as the long and short of it. Collins was tall and thin, his quiet competence towering almost a foot above Peach's squat pugnacity.

'As you say. Well, he'll be off next week. Apparently they've a crisis over Preston way.' He spoke as if it was at least a continent away, rather than ten miles. 'His replacement may be in later this week. Starts officially next Monday.' He looked at Peach then, and he could not prevent a small smile flickering across the lower part of his face. Percy found it most disconcerting. It was as if a toy poodle had suddenly bared its teeth.

'Do we know the officer, sir?'

'No. At least I don't myself.' Again there was that disturbing smile, as if he was aware of a joke that hadn't yet been revealed to the man in the armchair opposite him. Percy began to feel uneasy.

'We do have a name then, sir.'

'Oh yes, Percy. Your new detective sergeant will be called Blake.' Chief Superintendent Tucker steepled his fingers and looked at the fluorescent light fitting in the ceiling of his office as if it was the most intriguing and amusing thing in the world.

There was something going on here. Tucker hadn't even needed to consult his papers to find the name. And he was smiling again: it was quite eerie. Percy racked his brains for a few seconds but the name meant nothing to him. 'Might I know the officer's age, sir?'

This time Tucker did look at his papers. But he found the relevant one with unusual swiftness and certainty. In Percy's view, that meant the chief had been studying it carefully immediately before he arrived. He found this more than ever disturbing. Tucker said, 'Your new detective sergeant is only twenty-six, Percy. Recently promoted from DC, I believe, so clearly a promising officer. Probably be with you for quite a few years.' Tucker appeared to find this a deliciously diverting thought. When he finally brought his eyes back to a normal plane, he seemed surprised to find Peach still sitting meekly in his office. 'That will be all for now, Percy.'

For the first time, Tucker had called him 'Percy' throughout an interview. On his way back downstairs, Peach found that the most disconcerting thing of all.

On one thing, at least, Percy Peach would swiftly be reassured. The letter informing him that he had been accepted as a member of the North Lancashire Golf Club had been signed by the secretary and was already in the post for him. The last task of the day for the assistant in the club office was to type up the list of new members for display on the noticeboard of the club on the morrow.

In the committee room on the first floor of the club, the six men who constituted the Greens Committee were debating a change to the course which would have more far-reaching consequences than any of them could foresee on that quiet evening.

The chairman outlined the principles behind the proposal. 'Water is a feature of many good courses. Where it occurs naturally, we should make the most of it. Modern machinery enables us to do that. Our idea is to transform the stream which runs in front of the eighth tee into a small lake, perhaps sixty yards across and roughly circular.' He passed photocopies of a map of the suggested new hole round the table.

There were mutterings of approval, then the usual questionings about the cost such alterations would occasion. 'We would move the men's tee back and a little to the left, making the hole more of a dog-leg, so that players would have to drive over the new lake to the fairway. Once we'd dammed the stream in the valley, we should demolish one end of the old quarry and let the water drain away to the new lake. That would allow proper visibility from the tee and make the new hole a visual delight as well as a golfing pleasure.'

The head greenkeeper said, 'We could do most of the work ourselves. It would need a professional blaster to put a charge in one side of the old quarry, and a driver and bulldozer for perhaps two days. My lads could do the rest.'

The excitement grew as the project began to seem feasible. Someone said, 'The ladies wouldn't like it!' and there were a few chuckles; it was not clear whether this was a point in favour of or against the scheme. It was eventually pointed out that if the ladies' tee was left in its present place, it wouldn't be a very great carry for them across the new water. And for the elderly and infirm of both sexes, there would be a method of playing round rather than over the new lake.

So it was decided. The new lake and the longer hole were recommended to the full committee of the North Lancs. Within a week, they would accept the proposal. It all happened so swiftly that it seemed almost like unseemly haste to the older members among the decision-makers.

It was a change to the course which would have profound effects for several of the members. Including the newest one of all, Detective Inspector Percy Peach.

CHAPTER THREE

For Gary Jones, the early mornings were the best times of all. He thought there could be no better place in the world to be at six o'clock on a summer morning than a deserted golf course. He had fallen on his feet when he got the job here, far more than he realized at the time.

Dawn was coming later now of course, and the air was sharp with autumn cold. Soon the clocks would go back; it always felt as if winter wasn't far away when that happened. But it would be lighter for a while in the mornings and the trees in the lower parts of the course would be glorious mounds of colour in the still dawns. Gary looked forward to the changing seasons now. Until he came here, he had not been much aware of them.

He looked at the watch that he had bought with the first money he had saved from his own earnings. Twenty to eight. Only another twenty minutes to breakfast. He enjoyed the gatherings round the stove in the big shed, waiting for the kettle to boil and swapping news and banter with the other lads. When he had first come here on the YTS scheme, they had been a bit rough with him. You had to take the jokes about bananas and jungle bunnies when you were black, even when you had lived all your life here and never been farther than Blackpool. The difficult thing was pretending you hadn't heard them all before: people thought you were thin-skinned as well as black-skinned if you couldn't raise a laugh for them.

The worst of his tormentors had been the burly Charles Booth, whom he had once fought bitterly at school when he was only twelve. But the other green staff lads had taken Gary's side when Charlie tried to revive old memories. When Gary had proved himself a willing worker and been taken on to the staff properly after his YTS period was finished, they had accepted him as one of them.

Nowadays they all grumbled together about the members of the North Lancs and the stupid suggestions they made as they played the course. Each day they shared the tasks of raking the bunkers and mowing the greens and generally presenting the course as those same members would like it. As the head greenkeeper told them, 'There's plenty of daft buggers among them, I know, but they pay our wages each week, so grit your teeth and keep your head down. If in doubt, smile and say nothing.'

Gary liked his boss. Tommy Clarkson, the Head Green-keeper, had taken him under his wing from the early days, when he had known nothing about the work and had to be shown everything. One Saturday morning, when Mr Clarkson and Gary had been the only ones working, doing three hours' overtime getting the greens cut ready for a competition, the boss had done a wonderful thing. When they had finished their work on the course and the first members were driving off from the first tee, he had invited young Gary into his neat little cottage beside the course. He had been given breakfast, and eaten it with Mrs Clarkson and the three noisy children. Bacon and egg and sausage and tomato: Gary could still conjure up the image of his plate after three years.

From that day on, Tommy Clarkson's black labrador had taken a liking to Gary. It followed the slim figure every-where on the course, sometimes running exuberantly behind the little dumper truck with the broad tyres that the green staff used to get around the course, sometimes riding be-side him, chin on the side of the truck, pink tongue drooping from the side of his mouth in an expression of utter content.

The other lads had enjoyed seeing the two of them together. 'Come 'ere, you black bastard!' they'd shout, and
then, 'No, not you Gary, I meant the dog!' At least he hadn't
heard that one before, and had been able to laugh. After
that, he became one of the lads, even daring in due course to
tease them as vigorously as they did him. And on Saturday
afternoons, they went to the match together, trudging
through mean streets to the fine new stadium Jack Walker's
money had built for his beloved Rovers. They chanted
'Shearer! Shearer!' with ten thousand others, a unified East
Lancashire tribe, roaring home his goals, wearing the shirts
their heroes wore on the field.

When they came back to work on a Monday, they were a
good working team, the five of them. And it was the nature
of the job that you could always get away from the others, if
you wanted to; the wide open spaces of the golf course
meant that you were working on your own for quite a lot of
the time.

Gary was surprised how much he enjoyed the work. After
the first few months, he had started to ask questions about
fertilizers and weedkillers and why they were used at particular times of the year. Nowadays, Tommy Clarkson
explained everything they were doing to him, as they hol-
low-tined the greens and treated the surrounds to kill the
worms and sought out the tunnels where the moles made
their secret progress.

Tommy had said last week that he thought that if Gary
kept up his interest he might get promotion in a year or
two. He had even said that he thought he might have the
ability to become in due course a head greenkeeper himself,
if he kept on working and learning. Gary had never even
thought of anything like that but Tommy said there was no
reason why he shouldn't be ambitious. He'd have to learn
how to give orders to the other lads but that would come
easier as he got older. He was trying to get Gary on a course
at the Greenkeepers' Institute in March, but he wasn't to say

anything yet to the other lads, in case it caused trouble in the camp. Tommy Clarkson would tell them about it, when the time was right.

Tommy usually went home to his cottage for his break-fast break but he was still in the tractor shed when Gary and the other lads came in from the different parts of the course on this bright September morning. He was raising the blades a fraction on the gang mowers, which were used to cut the fairways behind the big blue tractor.

Clarkson looked up from the task when all his assistants were in the hut and the frying pan and the battered old toaster were overlaying the prevailing smell of oil with their own distinctive scents. 'Could be some overtime for you hungry lads, in the run-up to Christmas.'

There was immediate interest, as there always was at the mention of extra money. A bit of time and a half wouldn't come amiss in October and November. It was in the au-tumn, when the grass ceased to grow and the routine tasks of maintaining the course took less of their time, that the overtime usually died away to nothing. The basic wage of the assistants was quite low, especially for the two of them who were married with babies. It was one of them who said, 'What's happening then, boss?'

'Going to re-shape the eighth, aren't we?' Tommy Clark-son couldn't keep the satisfaction out of his voice. The changes had been his suggestions in the first place, though he had learned enough about the ways of the world to allow the chairman of the Greens Committee to put them for-ward as his own scheme to his fellow-members.

'Make it longer?'

'Make it longer, and make it more of a dog-leg. And make it the only hole on the course with water to carry from the tee. More variety, you see.' Tommy Clarkson was proud of his course. *Golf World* had called the North Lancs 'one of the best three inland courses in the North of England'. And Tommy knew it was one of the best kept: he never boasted but he had the confidence of a man who was on top of his job.

Gary said, 'How're we going to do that, boss?'

'With a little help from modern machinery, a little knowhow, and by the sweat of our brows. Well, mainly the sweat of your brows, actually, lads, under my expert super-vision. Hence the overtime.' He grinned round at the expectant faces as they digested his news, then was sur-prised by the dismay on the darkest of them.

Gary Jones said, 'How shall us make this lake, Mr Clarkson?' His Lancashire speech was always strong with the lads, asserting his right to be one of them. He did not often give his mentor his formal title nowadays: perhaps it was a reflection of the anxiety he felt.

Clarkson looked at him curiously; he had expected noth-ing but enthusiasm for his news. 'We shall build a dam across the stream which runs across the dip in front of the tee. There's plenty of loose stone there from the old quarry. We shall be building a new tee behind that quarry so that the little lake we shall make will be directly between it and the fairway. The maximum carry from the back tee won't be more than a hundred and fifty yards. Even you buggers'll be able to make that!'

There were some chuckles around the shed as Gary went to attend to the frying pan on the aged electric ring. Tommy was a good golfer, who had been down to four in his time. His assistants, who got cheap golf as one of the perks of the job, were at various stages of golfing development. Gary, with the suppleness of youth in his slim frame, had a fluid swing which hit the ball great distances, but not always in the direction he intended. He said as casually as he could, 'Won't the old quarry be in the way of the drive from the tee, boss?'

'Good thinking, young 'un. The members of the North Lancs don't like blind drives. So we shall move the bloody quarry! It won't be difficult, with the wonders of modern technology brought in to help us.' That was the phrase he always used when the club thought it necessary to supplement its own resources of manpower and machinery.

Gary said stupidly, 'Move the whole bloody thing?'

Tommy was glad to be able to air his comprehensive grasp of the scheme. 'It won't be difficult. One charge of explosive at the lowest point of the old quarry, to blast it away and let the water out.'

Gary did not have to ask the question this time. It was the deputy to Tommy Clarkson who said, 'Won't it mek a right mess of that area, boss? With all t' water and earth?'

'It will for a little while, yes. But we shall have a bulldozer in for as long as is necessary to do the real earthmoving and the levelling. The water in the old quarry pond will run straight down the hill into our lake. We shall use the stone we dislodge to build up the dam to the height we want. The earth we shall level and sow with seed. If we can get on with it quickly before the winter rains, it shouldn't look too much like the Somme.'

Gary said, 'But – but don't we need permission to do things like this from the authorities? Altering the landscape, like?'

'All been done, lad. County surveyor looked at it when he went round with me in the summer. Said it would constitute an improvement to the environment and a greater amenity. They like phrases like that, them environmental planners.' Tommy rolled out the title with reverence, not the contempt he might have used a few months earlier. His eldest son had just applied for an Environmental Studies course at college.

Gary said, 'So the old quarry pond is going to disappear altogether?'

Clarkson thought he had already made that quite clear. The black lad was usually quicker than this. He said, 'Within a month, if we're lucky and the weather helps us. Straight after the Autumn Scratch Medal is the plan.' It was the last serious competition of the golfing year.

Gary Jones did not eat a lot of breakfast after the boss had gone off to his cottage. He sat uncommunicative in the corner of the shed, anxious to be out on the course and alone with his thoughts.

Chief Superintendent Tucker came upon Detective Inspector Peach in the car park of the Brunton nick at Friday lunch-time. The DI was gazing at the chief's new Rover with a covetous air. That was not typical behaviour and Tucker should have been warned by it.

Instead, he said, 'Nice motor, isn't she, Peach?' and ran his fingers over the sleek maroon wing before fitting his key into the lock.

Percy started as though he had been stabbed, though he had been well aware of Tucker's approach behind him. He looked at the car as if seeing it for the first time. 'Er, yes, I suppose it is quite nice, sir. Can't say I'd really noticed, though. I was looking at the golf clubs on the back seat, you see. Nice to have time for a game during the week.'

He managed to make the casual words ring like an accusation in Tucker's ear, not least because he was bound straight for Brunton Golf Club and an afternoon fourball. The super said grandly, 'One of the rewards of office, Peach.' But he could not quite bring off the lordly disdain that would show he was not nettled.

Peach nodded. 'I feel I might be a tolerable player, if I could only get more time for the game.' He sighed mournfully and turned away.

Tucker, looking for a taunt in response, said, 'I think they expect quite a high standard at the North Lancs. Perhaps you should have been a bit less ambitious. Haven't heard about your membership, yet, I suppose?' Even as he delivered the question, he felt suddenly that it was a mistake, that he had somehow been led into it by the entire innocent exchange.

Percy said, 'Oh, I heard about that a couple of days ago, sir. Just a formality, as I think I suggested to you the other day. I'm in all right. Quite looking forward to a round on a decent course. When my duties permit it, of course.' He was away into the building before Tucker could even attempt to force out his congratulations.

On the Friday of that week, Peach bade an uncharacteristically fond farewell to the detective sergeant who had been his diligent supporter for three years.

During that time, he had delighted in referring to the tall, taciturn DS Collins as 'that long streak of discretion', but he realized now how well they had complemented each other in their methods. Collins had sometimes had to work to retain his dignity in the face of Percy's apparent contempt but he had never lost his composure. It had been a valuable quality, whilst he was working with an inspector who went for villains like a pit bull, and sometimes made his mind up on scanty evidence about who the villains were.

Peach openly despised sentiment, but he realized on the day of Collins's departure how much he was going to miss the miserable old bugger. 'No need to tell you to keep your nose clean, Fred – you're a bloody expert at that. But all the best, lad. It was time they made you up to inspector.'

From him, this was lavish praise, and Collins knew him too well to risk spoiling the moment by modest self-deprecation. He said simply, 'We were a good team, Percy, you and me. Got results.'

It was one of the rare occasions when both of them had fallen into the weakness of first names.

They had a little presentation in the CID section, then went off to the pub to mark the occasion of Fred's departure. On their way there, whilst they were still out of the range of other police ears, Percy said, 'Do you know anything about this bloke Blake who's coming in to replace you?' He had left it until the last possible moment because it seemed a weakness in him to ask. Any admission of anxiety would tarnish his rough-hewn image.

Fred said, 'Nothing at all. Don't you?' But he turned his face away, to avoid revealing the tiny smile he could not quite conceal. Rumour had whispered one astounding fact to him about his replacement but, if Percy hadn't found out, he was certainly not going to be the one to tell him. It was not like Peach to be so ill-informed about things which concerned him.

'I know bugger-all. He's a transfer from another force, apparently. I got the impression that Tommy Bloody Tucker knew more than he was telling me, though.'

'Boot's on the other foot from the usual, then, is it?'

It was true that Percy preferred to keep the super in the dark about his progress and methods whenever he could. But surely Tucker was not capable of some sort of revenge?

As they went into the pub, Percy felt his first shaft of real apprehension.

Paul Capstick was an efficient secretary of the North Lancashire Golf Club. Moreover, he believed in giving his members all the information he could, as quickly as he could. In his opinion, rumour fed on ignorance, and rumour could do much damage to the spirit of a golf club.

On the morning after the full committee had confirmed the recommendation to alter the eighth hole, he pinned up a typewritten account of the details on the main noticeboard, together with a map of the proposed new eighth hole, with its new men's tee and lake. The more detail he could announce, the more it would keep the members and their questions out of his hair.

It did not keep everyone away, of course. In the middle of the afternoon, the Ladies' Captain came breezily into his office. 'Sorry to bother you, Paul. You can guess why I'm here. On behalf of the female dinosaurs, who think any change to the course must be the beginning of Armageddon.'

Paul did not mind being interrupted by Christine Turner. After the harridans he had dealt with in his time, she was a positively refreshing presence in his office on a Friday afternoon. She perched her neat bottom on the edge of the spare desk he kept next to his and said, 'Just chew the fat with me about the new hole and then I'll go and reassure them. They use me to fire their bullets but at least that keeps you out of their firing line.'

Capstick was ready with the answers to allay female fears. 'The ladies' tee won't be moved back with the men's. I estimate the carry over the new lake for the ladies won't be more than eighty-five yards.'

'Is there anywhere they can bale out if they don't fancy it? We have one or two octogenarians, you know. Shame if they can't play for as long as they are able to.'

'No problem. We have quite a few male geriatrics as well, you know, even if you are the stronger sex. Let me show you.' Paul got out his copy of the map and she came over and bent her head beside his. The perfume was a vast improvement on the stale cigar smoke of his last visitor. 'There's a flat area just here, to the right of where the lake will be and short of the stream. It's a little to the right of the present fairway but all we'll need to do is mow out rather farther. Anyone who doesn't fancy driving over the lake, male or female, will have the safe option of knocking the ball down there and playing round the water rather than over it.'

'That's all I wanted to hear. I'll go and nip things in the bud before you get a deputation at your door.' At the secretary's suggestion, she took a couple of photocopies of his map, so that she could demonstrate the solution to her ladies as he had to her. Then she bustled away.

Paul Capstick was fifty-three. He wondered if it was a susceptible age. He had actually been quite sad to see a ladies' captain departing from his office so briskly.

Christine Turner chatted with her ageing ladies and enjoyed a pot of tea with them. She had the gift of enjoying most people's company, which meant in turn that most of them enjoyed hers. At a sprightly forty-five, she had seemed to these elders of the club a very young appointment to the highest office among the ladies, but she was rapidly winning them over. The four of them who had tea with her pronounced her quite charming when she eventually left them to their gossip.

As she went out through the foyer of the club, she noticed a figure studying the noticeboards which was vaguely familiar to her. She went over and interrupted his perusal. 'It's Derek, isn't it?'

She scarcely knew him. But she had known his daughter rather too well.

He turned his lean face to look at her. 'It's Mrs Turner, isn't it? Nice of you to stop.'

'Not at all. Are you playing much these days?' It was the standing golfing question but she put it awkwardly to him, because of the circumstances.

He smiled with an infinite sadness, as if he both understood that she was trying to help and knew that it was not possible. 'Not very much. I don't like leaving Shirley, you see.'

'She's still feeling very low, then? It's understandable.'

'Physically, she's all right. But she – she won't take an interest in anything.' His voice trembled a little.

She didn't want him to break down here, in this public place, for his sake, not hers. She said desperately, 'There's no news of Debbie, then?' At least she had remembered the name. But then she had no excuse for forgetting it, after the row they'd had, three days before she disappeared.

Derek Minton did not answer her question. He turned abruptly back to the noticeboard. 'Do you know anything about this?' he said, gesturing at the secretary's notice and the map beside it.

His voice was harsh but she understood that he did not

wish to talk about his daughter. Christine explained the principles of the development as patiently as she had just done to her octogenarians. 'It should be a good hole for you men from the new tee. A vast improvement, I'd – '

'What's going to happen to the old quarry?'

His voice rasped out the question. She did not mind him interrupting her, because he was so plainly under stress, but she found it unnerving that he stared not into her eyes but over her head. She said, 'It's to be drained, I think, and the ground evened out.'

'When?'

'As soon as possible. Derek, if you'd like me to sit with Shirley whilst you get away for a bit, come down here for a game, I'm sure I can – '

'There's no need. She can be left quite safely. It's just that she won't accept . . .' He shrugged hopelessly, supposing that she comprehended his meaning, not caring if she did not.

She left him staring again at the noticeboard. She wished she could restore to them the daughter that was gone. But in her heart she knew that she could offer no comfort: the girl was dead.

When she reached the double door of the club, she heard Derek Minton call from thirty yards behind her, 'Thank you, Mrs Turner.'

CHAPTER FOUR

Percy Peach played his first round at the North Lancs on the Sunday morning. It was not a happy experience.

He began with an extravagant slice from a first tee which was surrounded by members waiting to play. There were probably no more than twelve of them but they felt like twelve hundred to Percy in the stunned silence which followed his drive. He would not admit to any frailty so human, but he was in fact nervous. His round deteriorated accordingly, even from the low base of its beginning. His partner explained the changes planned to the eighth hole as they played it but by that time Percy was in no condition to digest the information; he comprehended only that an already difficult hole was going to become impossible. Even the powerful tinctures of the nineteenth hole brought only a partial recuperation.

On the Monday morning following this chastening experience, the last person he would have chosen to meet in the high-walled confines of the police station car park was Superintendent Tommy Bloody Tucker. But life was a bugger, so Tucker was waiting for him. Tommy asked whether he had played golf at the weekend, and for a moment Percy thought that he had somehow discovered the details of his disaster. But when Percy said, 'I enjoyed the challenge of the new course; some fascinating holes, and not a bad one around,' the chief did not snigger and come back with a barbed rejoinder, as he should have done.

Perhaps he had just been trying to be pleasant. Percy

found that possibility much more disturbing than his first thought. They went up in the lift together and Tucker left him with an injunction to 'enjoy his day' and a look that said more plainly than any words that he was sure Percy would not do so.

A strange, almost unnerving, thing happened to Peach when he went into the CID section. A silence fell most noticeably on the big, untidy room. Although there were nine people in it, all conversations stopped at his entry. He said to the girl on the switchboard, 'Has Detective Sergeant Blake arrived yet? He starts officially today.'

'Locker room, sir. Settling in.' The telephonist was a blonde, blue-eyed girl, who should have brightened his Monday morning, but today she did not look at him, seemed, indeed, to have difficulty in delivering the information before she became intensely busy with an incoming call.

He went and looked in the locker room, but there was no one there, apart from a detective constable who was putting on a clean shirt after what looked like a heavy night of passion. 'Seen DS Blake?' he said. With the police penchant for seizing upon the obvious, he expected they'd soon be calling the man 'Sexton' – surprising that he hadn't already acquired the nickname, in fact. The bloke had better not make a habit of being this elusive.

He was in his office, poring over a report from a Saturday evening drugs raid, when the evasive presence was finally made manifest.

A voice said curtly to the shining bald head above the desk, 'Detective Sergeant Blake, sir.'

'About bloody time, too!' said Percy. Might as well begin with some discipline. Be a bastard to start with: it was easy enough to relax later if you chose to.

Then something in the tone made him look up sharply.

'What the hell's this?' he shouted. It was definitely a shout, even in his own ears. He could not control it.

'It's a woman, sir.' The voice was cool, unamused, studiously neutral. 'Reporting for duty. Detective Sergeant Lucy Blake.'

Peach found himself on his feet before he realized he had moved. But it was outrage, not chivalry, that raised him so abruptly. 'What the 'ell's going on?' he snarled. The native Black Country vowels which had been submerged for years came leaping out under stress.

'That's what I'm here to find out, sir. I understand I'm to work closely with you.'

'Like hell you are! I can't work with a bloody woman!' He glared at her, willing her to shrivel before him like the pimply youths he regularly reduced to pools of grovel. She did not. She stared steadily back at him, unsmiling but watchful, awaiting his next move. He said belatedly and uselessly, 'No offence, love, but – '

'I understand we have to work with whoever those on high decide we should, sir. The choice is not ours but theirs. That was what I was told when I queried this particular arrangement.'

She stood erect but not quite at attention, almost exactly as tall as he was, not four feet from him. She had red hair and dark blue eyes which were set deep in a face which seemed to Peach at this first meeting to be framed to annoy him. The wide mouth gave no hint of either humour or annoyance. The light tweed jacket she had worn for this first meeting in plain clothes hung open, as it was meant to be worn. The breasts rose and fell gently beneath the light woollen sweater, but regularly, with no sign of passion or outrage. A cool one, this. Percy became aware that she had closed the door carefully behind her when she came in, so that this exchange should not be overheard by others.

She had expected trouble, then. And she was more prepared for it than he was.

He felt suddenly ridiculous, fuming without effect so close to this calm opponent. It would have been different if he had elicited some reaction, whether of outrage or of tears. If she would only shout back, he could bounce off that. This woman, with her understated resistance, her suggestion of an athletic frame beneath the demure clothes, her cool temperament in the face of his anger, suddenly reminded him of women cricketers and hockey players that he had played with in charity matches. It was not a comparison that was helpful to him at the moment.

He became aware that he must turn his wrath elsewhere. She wasn't responsible for this, any more than he was. They were both victims. He said abruptly, 'Get yourself some coffee, Detective Sergeant Blake. I'll let you know when I want you.'

For the first time, she hesitated, and he felt a little lift at the sight. He barked, 'That's an order, Sergeant Blake. The first one I've given you. And with any luck at all for both of us, the last!'

She looked at him for a second which seemed much longer, then turned abruptly and walked out, shutting the door as carefully behind her as when she had entered, denying him the satisfaction of a slam.

Percy went back to his desk and sat down. For two minutes he studied the harmless yellow wall opposite him unblinkingly, listening to his breathing returning slowly to normal. Then he went out of his office, ignored the lift, and leapt up the steps two at a time, until he reached the hardwood door of Superintendent T Tucker's room. He rapped the mahogany, did not even wait for the display from the column of lights, and marched in. The words began to pour before he had even crossed the threshold: 'It's not on, sir! I'm not going to stand for – '

His words stopped as abruptly as his stride checked. He was left comically off balance, stumbling from foot to foot in the centre of the room. In the armchair he had been invited to occupy himself on his last visit sat Sergeant Lucy Blake. She looked up at him and at last volunteered her first smile. It was small, but there was no doubt that it stemmed from amusement. It was as welcome to him as a lurcher's snarl.

Peach said, 'But I told you – '

'To get myself some coffee, yes. It's on the way. Superintendent Tucker was kind enough to offer me some.' Lucy Blake looked up interrogatively at the man behind the big, empty desk and he took his cue.

'Indeed I did. Must try to make the newcomer feel at home, mustn't we, Percy? As you have arrived so precipitately among us, I suppose I should ask you to join us.' Before Peach could deny him the pleasure, he pressed the intercom and said to the speaker, 'Would you put another cup on the tray, please? Detective Inspector Peach has ascended among us unexpectedly.'

Peach found himself sitting in the chair next to Lucy Blake before he knew it had happened. He had never seen Tucker so in control of a situation, so patently enjoying that control. The bastard must have been getting ready for this all last week. His series of knowing looks and smug rejoinders fell into place at last. Percy summoned his resources of control, made himself speak calmly, began with the phrase the man must surely detect as an irony, 'With the greatest of respect, sir, I must protest in the strongest – '

'Protest, Percy?' Tucker sprang upon the word he had clearly been waiting to hear. 'One at a time, please. Sergeant Blake was here first, and I'm not at all sure that in these situations rank should carry any precedence. My door is always open as you know, and whilst it is regrettable that you should both feel the need to complain – '

Peach ignored Tucker in his indigation as he twisted ninety degrees to confront the woman next to him. 'You, making a protest? I send you out to get a coffee and you come running up here – '

'Even faster than you ran yourself! That's what's getting to you, isn't it? You're such a pompous little chauvinist that you couldn't even see that you were being insulting. I was warned about you but I was prepared to make my own judgements, not rely on gossip. Well, it seems you're as blinkered and bigoted as those who have worked with you said you were. So I'm objecting to working with you. I want out.'

'That's enough!' said Tucker. 'I'm here to listen to complaints, but I won't stand for insubordination.'

But he had heard her out without interruption, thought Percy, and he didn't sound unduly displeased by her attack. That was undoubtedly true, for Tucker now said, 'I shall investigate your complaint, of course, Sergeant Blake, and if I find it justified I shall take appropriate action.' He glanced at Peach with undisguised pleasure, like a butcher just given the go-ahead to put down a vicious bull.

Peach articulated each syllable carefully as he said, 'No doubt you will be prepared to listen to my complaint just as carefully, sir. You're well known for your sense of fair play and your ability to take an objective view.'

Tucker looked at him suspiciously but Percy kept his eyes upon the wall behind the man's head, concentrating furiously, aware now that he must be careful to sound a note of reason. 'I should like to make it clear from the start that I have no personal complaint against DS Blake.' He ignored the snort of derision from beside him. 'I do not know where that notion could have come from. No, what concerns me, as always, is simply getting the job done as well as we possibly can. I think my methods have proved themselves over the years. But serious crime is dangerous work – more dangerous with each passing year, regrettably. There is no room in the work I do for a female detective sergeant, I'm afraid.'

'Why?' The word came like a pistol shot from the woman beside him. Her face was flushed. A lock of red hair had fallen over her forehead and the blue eyes glittered with fury.

Tucker held up a magisterial hand to her. 'I'll handle this,

Sergeant, if you don't mind. But the lady has a point, Inspector Peach. Our masters have long since admitted women to the processes of detection. There are even female detective inspectors.' He smiled encouragingly at Lucy Blake, then with a triumphant blandness at Percy Peach. His archness was terrible to behold. 'So why should even so effective an officer as DS Peach see himself as an exception to the rules we are all happy to operate by?'

Tucker was pleased with his delivery of the speech he had worked on over the last week. As Peach threatened to explode, the superintendent's civilian secretary brought in a tray with a pot of coffee, a plate of biscuits, and china cups and saucers. Tucker produced what he later decided was his master-stroke, a truly amazing improvisation. 'Perhaps you'd be kind enough to pour the coffee, Percy? We can't be seen to be sexist in the presence of the newest recruit to our team, can we?'

Peach's black eyebrows beetled so far forward that Lucy Blake could not see the dark, porcine pupils beneath them as he handed her a cup and saucer. 'Make the most of this,' he rasped. 'You'll find it's chipped mugs in the real world downstairs.'

In that moment, he knew that his cause was lost.

DS Blake bit into a ginger biscuit with her perfect white teeth, then raised her china cup to Percy in what seemed to his suspicious eyes an ironic toast. 'Thank you, sir. I expect I shall survive, though.'

CHAPTER FIVE

The first day of October might have been designed to show off the advantages of the North Lancashire golf course.

The Indian summer which descends in most years for at least a week in early autumn had chosen to fall this time upon the whole of Britain. From Caithness to Cornwall, the sun shone unfiltered by clouds as the days shortened and the country basked in the year's last warmth like a vast luxuriating animal. There were thin, still mists in the morning about the lower parts of the green land but as the sun rose and banished them the visibility on these mornings was the sharpest of the year.

Gary Jones looked out on the many miles of country he could see from the high ground around the eighth tee and congratulated himself again on the marvellous luck which had sent him here. To some of the older members, there was something incongruous in seeing a black man smelling the cool English air with such relish. But his fellow-workers, catching Gary's Lancashire accent as strong as theirs and knowing how he had grown up in nearby Brunton, saw nothing strange in the sight, though they liked to mock Gary's enthusiasm when it grew too bold for them.

Today he was strangely quiet. But even the least poetic soul would have paused over the view of the Ribble Valley from here. The land stretched away to Longridge Fell with only an occasional glimpse of the river and its tributaries. The bright green capping of the cupolas of Stonyhurst College was placed as if by a painter as a point of interest in the middle distance. The miles of land on either side of the broad, shallow valley were divided by the hedges and meadows of man, but not marked by his cities. Tommy Clarkson was prone to tell anyone who would listen that there was no town of any great size between here and Scotland to the north, despite the invisible proximity of Lancashire's industrial settlements to the south.

And away to the right was the great mound of Pendle Hill, with its associations with witches and the old faith which the area had held to long after Henry's breach with Rome. The land was wilder and bleaker here, with the great limestone heights of Ingleborough and Pen-y-Ghent sharp enough in the distance to persuade you that they were much nearer than they were. Gary had read that Penrith had once been capital of England, though he was not sure when that was and he had never been there. But he did know that this wild landscape to the north, which he looked at with his usual mixture of awe and pleasure, had not changed much in a thousand years.

Well, he and his fellows were making their own small amendment to the face of the earth here. There had been a couple of protests from members about the change, as there always were in these ecological days. But it had been explained to them that the quarry they were trying to preserve was itself an intrusion upon the landscape, of industrial origin and scarcely more than a hundred years' existence, and the protests had fallen apart.

As Tommy Clarkson sturdily maintained, what they would achieve in the next month or two would be an improvement to the area; the new small lake, sheltering in the lee of the hill, would be a more promising habitat for wildlife than the deep but tiny pool of the disused quarry. As the sun climbed higher and the blue of the sky above him became even more brilliant, Gary turned with a will to the building of the dam across the little stream that ran clear and sparkling from the only spring on this high ground.

It was satisfying work. One of his green staff colleagues had been brought up on a farm out beyond Clitheroe, and knew about the building of drystone walls. They had laid out their stones as he bade them by the side of the stream. Now, under his direction, the three young men selected and put into place the stones which they were gradually building into the lower section of the dam.

They had worked on it for the whole of yesterday. The wall was already eighteen yards long and two feet high, so that the members who came past them on this weekday morning could see the project beginning to take shape before their eyes. To Gary's secret surprise, the wall held back the water and the lake was beginning to build behind their handiwork. Moisture seeped through and re-formed into a tiny rivulet in the bed of the former stream, but that was the intention. When the lake was fully formed, the stream would both feed it and flow from it at the rate it had always done in its old course.

By the afternoon, the wall was three feet high and they had used almost all the stone they had gathered for the task. When they came back from their dinner break – in these northern climes lunch was a pretentious southern invention – the embryo lake was ten yards across, rising invisibly but inexorably towards the top layer of their dam. The first two of the many thousands of golf balls which would be lost here lay pathetically clear in the central section of the water.

Against the skyline, where the outcrop of the old quarry bulged above them, they saw three dark figures. They recognized the boss immediately, but the other two were strangers to them. Tommy Clarkson came and inspected their morning's work, complimenting Walter, the drystone-waller, on his achievement. The lad, unused to having a specialist skill to display, smiled shyly and shrugged away the praise, his boot kicking absently at the ground. 'We shall need more stone afore we can build much higher, boss,' he said, pointing at the scattered and mostly rejected stones which were all that remained of the several trailer loads they had brought here behind the tractor.

Tommy took off the cap he invariably wore and looked at the heavens, wiping his brow; it was a mannerism he often used as a prelude to speech. 'You shall have stone a-plenty before the day's out. Those chaps have come to plant a charge to blow away this side of the old quarry. The water should come tumbling down here and there should be plenty of stone up there after the blast.' They looked up to the two figures, who had already decided exactly where to place the charge and were determining how much explosive the enterprise would need.

Walter was dispatched with another of the assistants to bring up the tractor and trailer from the machine shed, and Tommy Clarkson took Gary up above the quarry with him to begin marking out the site of the new tee for this remodelled hole. They soon had the rectangle marked out with string and wooden pegs, but Tommy found his dark young protégé unusually silent. Gary kept sneaking glances at the movements of the two explosives experts on the ground below them, though for much of the time the men were out of sight behind the rugged outcrops of stone which marked the perimeter of the old workings.

Tommy Clarkson decided that Gary had probably never seen an explosion of this kind at close quarters. Few people had nowadays, unless you counted the demolition of the sixties council blocks which had become something of a spectator sport in the cities. 'All right, lad, we'll go and watch from the other side, when we've finished this,' he said indulgently. Gary grinned weakly, as though in apology for such an unprofessional attitude.

They had already erected the notices warning the members that the eighth hole was out of play for the afternoon. 'Come on!' said Tommy, 'before we miss the excitement!' Like all good greenkeepers, he was as thrilled as a schoolboy by any activity that promised a major improvement to this course. He did not notice how reluctantly Gary Jones trailed behind him.

It was an efficient explosion; not spectacular, by the standards of the professionals who engineered it, but satisfying in its effects. To Tommy Clarkson and Gary Jones, standing eighty yards away in the position of safety to which they had been directed, it was quite sufficiently dramatic.

There was a muffled but still quite loud bang, then a fountain of earth and stones, which flew like water into the clear air, appeared to hang against the blue sky for a moment, then fell to earth in a prolonged spatter of sound. There was a ragged cheer from the four green staff; the two experts treated this as no more than a routine part of the day's work. After a suitable interval of awe, Tommy Clarkson, who seemed to think it incumbent upon him as the senior man to make some comment, said, 'Just like the bloody Blitz!' He was far too young to have been even a child of the war but he felt the comment emphasized his senior status among the youngsters on his staff.

The excitement was not over. The charges had been well placed, and the water from the quarry was pouring through the livid gap which had been blown in the side of its containing wall. The brown torrent cascaded down the hillside in a sudden flood, frightening in its speed and volume even though no one stood in its path.

The flood raced down the cleft in the slope exactly as they had planned, joining the waters of the small lake they had already contrived, arriving like a tidal wave upon its still surface. The wave rushed across to the far bank of the natural container they had prepared for it, then fell back and eventually disappeared into a hundred subsidiary currents and disturbances. The residue began to pour over the top of the barrier they had made, but gently, subsiding in a moment into a series of rivulets. Walter said proudly, 'Our wall held firm, even against that lot!'

The hillside was now littered with a mixture of rocks, mud, earth and turf. The six men who had seen the explosion moved from their different positions to what a few minutes ago had been the old quarry pond. Most of the water had already gone, and the sides which had not seen the air for eighty years were exposed and raw on the near-vertical faces which remained intact. At the bottom of the steep-sided pit, there was still a muddy remnant of the pool, perhaps no more than two feet deep.

Even that would not survive long, for the force of the departing water had removed most of the earth at that shattered side of the pool, so that the ragged gap had become now a sea of mud, with no resistance against the remaining water. The brown water frothed out in a gentle stream, carrying the mud with it wherever it met resistance. In a few minutes, there would be no more than a series of puddles at the bottom of the quarry.

The detritus of the years began to emerge, surreal shapes covered in slime. Not much had been dumped here, since the quarry had been on private land, far from any road and hundreds of yards from public footpaths. There were two broken umbrellas, probably tossed there after their collapse by disgruntled golfers. There was what looked like a biscuit tin of thirty years or more before. There was a single bicycle wheel.

And as the last of the waters seeped away down the slope, there was something else entirely. Limbs splayed into an obscene spreadeagling by the weights which held them down, there was something that once had moved and spoken and laughed like other human things. The men who found it now were cast into a sudden silence. The thing which had once been human like them lay face upwards, but with its whole surface mercifully covered in slime, so that no one could distinguish features on the face to which six pairs of eyes were inevitably drawn.

Five of them were not sure at that first sighting whether

the thing had been male or female. But one of them knew.
All of them were aghast at the sight. But one of them was
not surprised.

CHAPTER SIX

As head of the CID section at Brunton, Superintendent Tucker heard about the discovery of a body on the eighth hole of the North Lancashire Golf Club within twenty minutes.

One of the tools of management essential to senior ranks is the capacity for delegation. It is a skill which is emphasized in all the management courses for high-ranking policemen. It was the one talent that Tommy Tucker had practised with real diligence. According to Detective Inspector Percy Peach, Tucker delegated all work and all responsibility until they disappeared from sight. In Percy's not entirely unbiased view, Tommy Bloody Tucker passed the buck as swiftly as if it was a red-hot turd.

Superintendent Tucker received the news of a decaying corpse of indeterminate age in the privacy of his penthouse office. He turned his swivel chair away from the window, with its view of the last two mill chimneys in the town and the rows of terraced housing snaking away over the hills from the centre. Then he looked at the emulsion-painted wall, which was blank apart from the small Lowry print which was his gesture towards his roots. He found the wall an aid to thought.

Within two minutes, his face brightened. Awkward case, this was going to be. Body still to be identified; location unhelpful; scene-of-crime evidence no doubt minimal; suspects very probably no longer in the area; scents long gone cold. No one was likely to make a reputation on the strength of this one. Tucker mentally ticked off the list, then smiled.

He picked up the internal telephone. 'Peach? Something interesting has just come in. Seems right up your street, especially with your specialist knowledge of the area where the body was discovered . . . Yes, there is a body. Oh, and Percy, you'll need to take DS Blake out there with you. Be a good run-in for the new pairing, this one will. You must have been looking forward to a serious crime investigation to test out the partnership.'

He put down the phone before Peach could harass him by demanding detail. Then he swivelled his chair back to enjoy the view over the town. It was an indulgence, but he knew he could not be observed: Tommy Tucker permitted himself his first chuckle of the week.

In his office at the North Lancashire Golf Club, the secretary strove to digest the sensational news from the course. Paul Capstick had not the wealth of experience of the darker side of life that made Superintendent Thomas Tucker such a model of composure. His reaction to the news of the corpse at the bottom of the old quarry pit was nothing like so measured as that of the head of the Brunton CID. 'Bloody hell!' was all he said to his female assistant. But he thought, 'Why here? Why me?'

It was an understandable response. The secretary of a golf club is accustomed to think in terms of his organization before he allows himself a personal thought. The popular press, confident of a conditioned reaction in its readers, likes to make fun of golf clubs, and television has of late enjoyed its own measure of hilarity at their expense. Over recent years, some clubs, though not Paul Capstick's, have provided the eager media with a wealth of comic social material.

Scandal is even better than laughter as a boost to audience figures, if it can be found in high places, and golf clubs are seen as bastions of privilege and citadels of reaction by many who do not play the ancient game. A body on the course is a sensational starting point; if in the weeks to come it proved to be connected with one or more of the members, the North Lancs could remain in the headlines until it acquired a notoriety.

That was not a pleasant thought for Paul Capstick. He quailed at the thought of fending off insistent, thick-skinned reporters. He groaned at the thought of distractions from his already busy schedule. This was sure to halt work on the modifications to the eighth hole, and just when the weather had seemed to be assisting them with the heavier and messier parts of the work. The members would not like that; and members had a habit of assigning all blame to the secretary, even when only the most oblique of logic would allow them to do so.

As Paul Capstick hurried out to the eighth hole, the future on this perfect October day seemed suddenly full of problems. It had been suggested to him that he put in an application for the secretaryship at Royal Lytham when that vacancy occurred in a year or so. The chairman at Royal Birkdale had even suggested that they might come head-hunting for him when their post fell vacant. Was all this to be thrown into jeopardy through unwanted publicity at the North Lancs?

Golf club secretaries grow used to looking ahead. It is right for them to do so. But it tends to make them nervous.

Paul found as he hurried out to the eighth that the police surgeon was already on the scene. He felt the first stab at his *amour propre* when he saw policemen roping off the area and beginning the erection of a canvas screen; it was the first time he could remember outsiders erecting such barriers on a golf course without any consultation with the secretary. But these, he told himself again, were unusual circumstances.

The police surgeon had put on a pair of wellingtons to wade into the mud and make his grisly examination. With the dark trousers of his city suit tucked carefully into the green rubber, he looked like a company director visiting a building site. When Paul Capstick called to the doctor across the twenty yards of brown water and oozing silt, he did it more to announce his presence than in genuine pursuit of information. 'Is it a suicide, do you think, Doctor Patterson?'

The police surgeon shook his head, bent again to his task, stooping over the body without moving his feet – there might be clues beneath them, even here. He said nothing until he had concluded this first brief ritual over the corpse. A death had to be officially certified, even in these bizarre circumstances, even at this remove from the last moments of life. He would have to begin his report by stating that these remains were indeed human. That there was material here for the coroner's court.

Capstick stood motionless with Tommy Clarkson at the side of the devastated quarry. Doctor Patterson did not bend for long over the thing at its centre. He waded carefully back through the puddles to the scarred grass beside them. 'No suicide ever weighted every limb like that before casting herself into the water,' he said.

'Herself?' Paul looked unwittingly at the slime-shrouded form which had once been human.

'That much I can say. But not yet how old she was. Mustn't disturb anything, you see. But I doubt whether this was a drowning.'

Already that thing beneath the slime was beginning to acquire an identity. Paul looked anxiously towards the spot where a policeman had stopped a little knot of members from approaching any nearer to them. 'Can we get the ambulance in now, and get this – get her away?'

The doctor shook his head. 'The ambulance will already have been ordered.' The meat wagon, the police called it, but there was no point in visiting that term upon the laity. 'But it will be some time before they can remove the cadaver, I'm afraid. The scene-of-crime team will need to examine the area thoroughly before anyone tramples over it. Anyone other than me, that is.'

He looked back ruefully over the path he had trodden to where the shape of the body poked from the residue of water, the weights still stretching and defining its limbs, as if they had been attached as a prelude to some ancient torture. The path of the police surgeon's journey to and from it was marked by a straggling line of small bubbles.

'But this may not even be the scene of the crime.'

'Very probably not, if this isn't a drowning. But there may be things around which give a clue to her killer, even at this distance. He may have dropped something into the pond with her. There may be bits of his hair or his clothing on hers, though I doubt they'll still be distinguishable after she's been under the water for all this time.'

'You say "he",' said Paul Capstick. He still felt as though this couldn't be happening to him. He had to keep looking back to the thing half-hidden by water and mud to convince himself that it was real.

Patterson laughed. 'You speak like a policeman, Paul. I made the assumption that most laymen would make that a man did this. But you're quite right, of course.' He glanced back at the shape to which he had just given a gender. 'There'll be more details after the autopsy, but she was probably quite slight. There's no reason why it shouldn't have been a woman who put her in there. Besides, for all we know, she could have been killed here at the edge of the pond, not carried here.'

He left them then, anxious to get back to the work of his practice after the diversion of this macabre sideline. Tommy Clarkson, sensing the secretary's disquiet at this unsuspected tragedy, did his best to divert him. 'At least we should be able to get on with the work down there.'

For the first time since his arrival, Paul turned to look down the slope at the scene below them. In more normal circumstances, he would have been thrilled to see the half-formed lake, forming and enlarging itself exactly as they had planned. The water was still now, and they could see the shape this new feature of the course would have when it was fully formed. Tommy said, 'We've got the tractor and trailer up here, ready to pick up this new stone as soon as we can. There should be enough to build the dam to about seven feet, which is the height we agreed.'

Ninety yards below them, Clarkson's four assistants were already using the rocks which the blast had scattered across the slope to put another layer on their half-built dam. Tommy looked at them for a moment with what might have been a pride in their handiwork. Then he voiced the thought which had been troubling him for the last hour to the man who was his immediate employer. 'One of the lads seemed a bit bothered by this.'

Capstick looked at him curiously. 'All of them would be, I should hope, Tommy.'

'No, not just that. I mean, before it – before this was found. Even before we started the work, he was worried about it, hoping that someone would change our minds and the whole scheme would be dropped.'

The two of them turned and looked at the group working steadily on the dam below them. Paul Capstick's mind was still reeling. It had enough to cope with, without taking this on. But he knew there was no escape from the knowledge, now that the head greenkeeper had gone this far. He said a little breathlessly, 'And which of your lads would this be, Tommy?'

'Gary Jones.'

As if responding to a cue, the slim figure below them stood erect for a moment from his work and looked anxiously upwards, towards the spot where the body lay waiting to give up its secrets.

There were too many people around a golf course for a secret to remain hidden for very long. Well before the grisly revelation at the bottom of the quarry pit, there was interest in the new earthworks which were re-shaping the eighth hole. Everyone around the place understood what the dull sound of the explosion at the old quarry was about. When police cars began to ease their way over the course half an hour later, the clubhouse was soon alive with the sensational news of a body discovered.

When intelligence of this kind is passed from person to person, each new recipient likes to add a new gloss in conveying the news to others. The scene at the site of the shattered old quarry, to which none of them were eyewitnesses, was imaginatively embellished with gruesome detail. And the word which no one at the scene of the discovery had cared to voice was soon being whispered in the clubhouse. Murder.

Christine Turner heard the word from behind the locked door of her cubicle in the ladies' cloakroom. It was not a dignified retreat for the ladies' captain of the North Lancs. She could not remember hiding in a lavatory since she had gone there to sulk and to plan as a child. But it was the only place in the club where she could guarantee that she would not be disturbed.

She sat there, alone with her tumbling thoughts, trying to put some sort of organization upon them. And then two women came into the cloakroom, their voices alight with excitement, full of the vicarious animation of dramatic events which have no close connection and therefore no real fear. 'It's a woman, they say,' said the first, 'and almost certainly a sex crime.' Rumour's insidious tongue was rapidly turning conjecture into fact for her.

'Murder,' said the other, in awed tones. Then, having tried out the word and found it satisfactory, she reiterated it in capital letters. 'MURDER! And on our course. Wonder what the committee will make of that at the annual general meeting?'

They giggled together for a moment at the delicious

picture. Then the first one said, 'Have we any idea who it is yet?'

'No. Apparently no one knows yet how long she's been in there. None of our members have gone missing, have they?'

'Not that I know of. But I can think of a few male members who might be candidates for murderer.' They laughed delightedly at the thought, but didn't suggest any names. Perhaps they had become aware of the single closed door in the cubicles behind them. They agreed to order tea and went off to await further news from the course.

Christine Turner sat for a while longer in her self-imposed cell, trying to compose herself to face the world outside it. She told herself she was being totally illogical about this. There was no real evidence to support her wild fears.

'Not yet', that other, insistent voice within her said. 'Not yet.'

All that was established was that a body had been found. The body of a woman. Not even a young woman, as far as she knew. The corpse could have been put there last week, for all that had been said so far. The woman might never have lived round here, might have had no connection with the area. In all probability, Christine had never seen this victim when she was alive.

It was no good. In her heart, Christine Turner was convinced that she knew exactly who this was.

Derek Minton took care to arrive in the house at his usual time. He could not have explained why, but he thought that might be quite important to both of them in what was to come.

He had heard the news an hour before he finished work. In the council offices, news spread fast, and the block housing the police headquarters was within two minutes of them. This was the area of the town where over the last fifteen years new municipal building had replaced the huddled terraces and high-chimneyed mills of King Cotton. Since the first hushed whispers of the discovery of a woman's body on the North Lancashire golf course had reached him, Minton had moved like one in a trance, his emotions held in a numbed suspension, his fingers completing the routine tasks on the paperwork in front of him with a competence that was inexplicable. He did not realize that the end of the working day was at hand until chairs around him on the floor where forty people worked together began to shuffle and the locks turned in desk drawers and filing cabinets.

He walked home, hoping to clarify his thoughts over the forty minutes it took him, trying to plan what he would say to Shirley. He was not successful. The sun was still bright in the October sky, even as it dipped towards the roofs of the long rows of semi-detached houses between which he walked. Women and a few retired men were working in some of the front gardens, pausing frequently to gaze up at the clear blue sky and congratulate themselves on their good fortune. Weather like this was worth a comment as Lancashire moved into autumn, and more than one of the occupants called 'Lovely day!' to him as he walked briskly beside the low walls and privet hedges.

It was that sort of afternoon, the sort which made people glad to be alive and anxious to communicate that enjoyment to others. Yet all the while he could picture only the little gang of watchers around that place on the golf course. His route lay in that direction: his house could not be much more than a mile from the North Lancs.

When he had first married Shirley, in those first happy days when she rejoiced to be with him and he was coming to terms with acquiring a ready-made family, they had often walked over the path which skirted the high part of the course. Shirley would sometimes slip her hand into his as the children danced impatiently ahead, their high voices shrilling with excitement, as though competing with the larks which rose in such numbers from the rushes and heather on the ground around them.

He had asked himself too often why it had all gone wrong to repeat that fruitless query now. If he had walked home along the main road, where his bus normally took him, he might have met the ambulance coming from the course. That is if they used an ambulance on these occasions; he was vague about that, his only knowledge coming from television crime series. He never read about crime, whether real or fictional.

At least Shirley was not looking at Debbie's photograph when he went into the house. He had had a premonition that she would already have heard his news, but of course she had not. He wondered as he looked at her how he could ever have conceived that idea. Probably the news had not reached the Radio Lancashire bulletins yet but, in any case, Shirley did not have the radio on nowadays. And the neighbours had long since given up the effort of speaking to her. Conversations needed two sides, even if one of them only listened.

The room was warm with the afternoon sun. Yet she who had once so loved the air had opened neither the window nor the patio door. Derek took off his jacket, folding it carefully over the back of a chair as he wondered how he could manage this. He said, 'How long until tea, love?'

'Have it when you want it. It's only bacon and egg. But I'll fry up the black pudding you brought home to have with it, if you like.'

He had never taken over the meals, even when she was at her worst. The doctor said it was a kind of therapy for her, though the doctor had never seen her moving like an automaton through the kitchen of which she had once been so proud. She cooked a meal for Derek each day, though sometimes the timing went a little awry: that was not surprising, he thought, when Shirley frequently had little awareness of what part of the day it was. She ate very little herself, even though she placed upon her plate the same portions she had always given herself.

He said, 'We'll leave it a little while then. I'll make us a cup of tea.' She looked up at him for a moment, then returned her gaze to the garden and its last golden glow of autumnal sun. Normally, he would have been glad to see a reaction in her. Today it made him apprehensive. He still had no idea how he was going to tackle this.

It was Shirley who pricked him into speech when he came back with the tea tray. She said, 'In three weeks, it will be exactly two years. Perhaps she'll come home then.' In the early days, she would have looked at him, hoping for some answering note of encouragement. For months now, she had delivered her thoughts as if they were parts of an intermittent monologue, requiring neither confirmation nor denial from him.

He leant forward and took her hand in his, trying not to notice the way she looked sharply down at his hands encasing hers, as if they belonged to a stranger and the action was unnatural. 'There's been a development, love.' So this was how it was going to be, he thought, seeing himself as though he stood in the doorway: wrapping it up, talking to her as if he was a professional counsellor, visiting once a week on paid duty.

She looked at him then, for the first time since he had come into the house. Although she said nothing, it was the nearest thing he could remember to a normal reaction in weeks. He wondered if some sixth sense was operating even through her cocoon of pain, to tell her that there was a crisis at hand. He said, 'They've found a body.'

The mind works in peculiar, sometimes unhelpful ways; he was beset at this inopportune moment by the thought of how useful were the anonymous 'they' to the English. Then he pressed on, 'It was in a pond, on the golf course. The North Lancs.'

Shirley nodded, looking out to where a thrush hopped at the far end of the lawn. He studied her profile; there was no sign of apprehension in it. Any sort of interest from her would be a bonus, he thought, with a sudden savagery which frightened him. In slow motion, as if she were anxious not to cause offence, she removed her right hand from between his and folded it demurely with her left one in her lap. With her unlined, expressionless face, she looked for a moment like a child on her best behaviour.

'It's a woman, Shirley. A young woman.' He couldn't remember whether he had heard this in the gossip at work, but he pressed it upon her none the less. The more circumstantial evidence he could offer, the greater his chances of breaking through. 'You've got to face it, this time. They might be coming to see us, you see. The police, I mean.'

How much easier it would be if there was some reaction from her, even if she screamed, or wept, or beat at him with her fists to release her agony. Something like that would have to come, if they were ever to get back to normal. For the first time, he realized that he welcomed the news he had to give her, because it might be the first step back to that normality. He must be under a lot of strain himself, to find this a relief.

He said quietly, pitching his voice as consciously as an actor seeking for a particular effect, 'I think they'll find it's Debbie, love.'

She said nothing, remaining motionless. For a moment, he could not be sure she had taken it in. Then she said, 'Not Debbie. It can't be Debbie. Not so close to home, after all these months.'

To an outsider, it would have been the same zombie-like monotone in which she had delivered so much else in the preceding weeks. It took someone who had listened as hard and as long as Derek to detect a change. There was to him the slightest note of rising panic, the faintest tinge of despair.

It was a crazy paradox that he should find in these things a spurt of hope.

He shifted a little nearer, taking both of her hands now in his. He was preparing to make a little concession, probing his way now into some new kind of relationship with her. It felt like that, like a new beginning. 'I may be wrong, I suppose. But you know that I've always felt that if Debbie was alive, she'd have been in contact with us. Even if it was just to let us know that she was safe. She'd have done that, you know, our Debbie. I'm sorry, love. I – I just feel this is Debbie, that's all.'

He had spoken quickly, wanting to get it all out before she could interrupt him, with her bland vision of a happy daughter who was alive and unharmed in some far-off, indeterminate place. She turned her head slowly to look at him, meeting his gaze for the first time in months.

Perhaps it was also the first time she had noticed the pain in his face. Whatever the reason, she moved her hands lightly up his forearms, until they stopped on the muscles below his shoulders. The touch of her fingers was light, investigative: as if they were lovers exploring each other for the first time, he would think later.

In a whisper so low that he would not have heard it if they had not been so close, she commanded him, 'Hold me, Derek.'

He wrapped his arms round her then, feeling her hair against his chin. It was not soft, as he had remembered it, but wiry, almost abrasive. With her face against his chest, he found himself suddenly weeping, then convulsed by a wild sobbing. He wanted to apologize, to explain how he knew he should be calm and consoling, a rock for her to fasten upon. But he was in no condition to frame words.

In a little while, her arms crept round to his shoulder blades. As his own sobbing subsided, he found that his shirt was wet with her tears.

CHAPTER SEVEN

P ercy Peach glared moodily at the back of Detective Sergeant Lucy Blake. It was an aspect he had grown familiar with during their short association.

He spoke to the sturdy shoulders reluctantly, for he was loath to share any information with them, as if doing so might in itself compromise his position. 'There's a body turned up at the golf course, apparently. We're to investigate it, Tommy Bloody Tucker says.' He felt oddly disorientated, knowing that the scent of a murder would normally have had him springing about like an excited terrier.

'Which golf course?' The response was as low-key as his revelation. She did not turn to face him, nor even look up from her desk.

'The North Lancs.'

'Ooh, there's posh! On home ground for you, then. Sir.' The last word came like an afterthought, an ironic, insulting appendage. She had looked up now from her papers, but she stared straight ahead of her, alert as a cat, still refusing to turn.

Lucy Blake's back, with its waist surprisingly trim above the more opulent contours beneath it, was proving increasingly disconcerting to Peach. He had seen a lot of it over the last few days, and for a while he had thought it would be fine by him if that was all he ever saw of her. But now he realized that it did not help his flow of invective. He needed a face to fasten his hostility upon, reactions to his barbs to encourage him to continue them. And he had not known that his new DS was aware of his status as a newly elected member of the North Lancs.

He said, 'Word is the body's been there for some time. It's a female, probably below the age of thirty-five. We shall know more after the PM.' He released the little information he had as grudgingly as a miser dispensing his gold. 'You'd better go and start the check on the local missing persons register, Sergeant.'

Lucy Blake stood up straight, looked at him briefly, and turned on her heel. Once she had gone, Percy leaned back on his seat, raising it on to two legs, straining back to the point where he was about to fall backwards, as he had been used to do as a boy when unobserved by adults. He had chosen the task he would have least relished himself for her. The bitch would be busy for the rest of the day at the computer screen, with luck.

He was almost balancing the chair on its two back legs, gingerly raising his feet from the carpet, when the door opened abruptly, without any prior knock. He had been concentrating so hard on his balancing act that the surprise was too much for him. He lost concentration and equilibrium in the same instant, disappearing backwards into the corner of the room in a welter of flying shoe-leather and turn-ups.

If Lucy Blake allowed herself any amusement at the sight, it had been removed from her features before Peach was able to inspect them. He said from the floor, 'What the hell? I told you to – '

'The computer search of local missing females is now in hand, sir, as you ordered.'

Percy scrambled first to all fours and then to his feet, the process being more laboured because he knew with what interest it was being observed. 'What I ordered, Sergeant Blake, was that you should conduct that research yourself. I did *not* suggest that – '

'Work for a detective constable, sir, I thought. DC Jackson is well used to such things. Was able to turn up the relevant files on the computer within seconds. He'll have the material you require with us in twenty minutes, he says. Far more quickly than I should have managed it. That's the advantage of a specialist. Meanwhile, I am at your service for whatever professional task you think appropriate.'

He dusted the seat of his trousers, so vigorously that his hand left a red weal on his buttock which he would examine with horror that evening. Fortunately for him, the phone shrilled at that moment, preventing him from making a suggestion to his sergeant that would undoubtedly have caused him further trouble. He snatched it up, modulating his snarling response when he found out the speaker. 'Right. Thank you. I'll come myself. We'll need an exhibits officer, of course.' He glanced across the room to where Blake was resuming her seat and allowed himself a small, vindictive smile. 'And I'll bring my new detective sergeant with me, I think.'

He was hoping she would ask him about the call, but of course she did not. He had to make the running himself, as usual. 'That was the pathologist. Autopsy on the cadaver tomorrow morning at eight-thirty. It's deteriorated badly, they reckon. Very nasty, to those not used to such things. But I don't suppose it will upset we professionals.'

'Us professionals, I think that would be, sir. I'll be there.' She looked towards the corner of the room, where the chair lay still on its side. 'Just in case you collapse under the pressure, sir.'

Even on this golden October day, there was not much light left now. And on the eighth hole of the North Lancashire, there were only policemen and their civilian acolytes.

There had been human killings within yards of this spot one thousand years and more before this night, and the scene which stretched away to the north over the last great outposts of the Pennines had not changed much in all that time. But these latest human occupants, moving ant-like over the shoulder of the hill, had no thought for those earlier deaths, nor for the bloodshed on these lonely fells in the intervening centuries. The death that concerned them might be insignificant against the cosmic backcloth of its setting but it occupied all the thoughts of the men who had to deal with it.

They had thought it best to bring in the Land Rover with its four-wheel drive to remove the remains. An ordinary ambulance would probably have made it across the close-mown turf in this weather, but there was no sense in risking spinning wheels. The thing they were removing had once been human, should have been duly mourned with its last rites at the time of the death. They would risk no last blow to its diminished dignity now.

Besides, the police these days were open to scrutiny and there were always those only too ready to criticize. Better not to give those mischievous tongues any cause for complaint about the procedures. And Detective Superintendent Tucker, who was watching over the operation as the officer in charge of this embryo case, was also anxious that there should be as little damage as possible to the hallowed turf of the North Lancs fairways, where many of the town's most influential feet were known to tread. This would be his only direct contact with the crime, so it was important to him that there should be no cock-ups.

The scene-of-crime team had finished their work now. They had gathered and bagged what they could from the bottom of the pond and the surrounding area. Once the corpse had been removed, they would use their floodlights for a final sift through the mud and earth which lay around and beneath the body and the stones which had held it static for so long. Anything else would wait for the morrow. There would be no invasion and no disturbance of this lonely site.

The men who moved gingerly into the slime at the bottom of the old quarry wore plastic gloves and face masks. The dead must be afforded what dignity was possible, but the living must be protected from the dangers of decaying flesh and the things which sometimes fed upon it. Under the direction of the pathologist, they lifted the dripping shape carefully on to a large polythene sheet and shuffled back over the treacherous and uneven route to the firmer ground at the side of the quarry, now browned by the tread of many feet over the preceding five hours. Once there, they drew the sides of the sheet together and sealed it.

With each step in the process, the burden became more anonymous, less human. Within minutes, it had been placed in the fibre-glass 'shell' and lost all definition. Unconsciously, the men relaxed and speeded up their movements, safe in the knowledge that their macabre subject was now less vulnerable and their task almost complete. The plain coffin was slid into the back of the Land Rover and the doors locked upon it. The vehicle moved cautiously away down the slope, speeding up a little as its lights picked out the way it had come over the flatter ground.

Save for a last faint glow in the west, over the point where Blackpool Tower had been distantly visible earlier in the day, the scene was now in darkness.

The water ran steadily over the stainless steel of the pathologist's cutting area, sluicing away the detritus of his work, signifying that all that was significant had been extracted.

Peach wrinkled his nose suggestively. 'Pongs a bit, don't she?' he said, studying his sergeant from the corner of his eye. She should have been green by now. Instead, she looked distressingly animated, with one lock of her dark red hair creeping unchecked over her forehead.

Lucy Blake said, 'I find the smell of the formaldehyde almost worse than the smell of the human decay it disguises. Matters of taste, I suppose. This has been very interesting: I've never seen the dissection of a body as far gone as this one before.'

If the pathologist was surprised at her coolness, he was

much too wise to refer to her gender. He said, 'Good to see someone taking such interest in the processes of science. Some officers find post mortems a bit much for their stomachs.' He looked to where the various elements of his dissections were laid out and labelled in bowls on the unit beside them, like items assembled for some nightmare buffet.

'When you've attended a few bad road accidents, this is child's play,' she said. 'So long as it's not alive, then it doesn't feel, and it can't be either helped or hurt. That's the way I look at it.'

Peach thought these two were far too cosy with each other. He wasn't quite sure what he had hoped for, but it had certainly included a fit of the vapours from his new sergeant. He said to the pathologist, 'Can you summarize your results for us, then, please? We have an investigation to get on with, you see.'

The doctor smiled, beginning to peel off his polythene gloves. Peach had a disconcerting notion that this man knew how the inspector's nose had been put out of joint: he certainly seemed both gratified and amused by Lucy Blake's resilience. 'I'll put it all in writing for you later today. It's all in here, as you know.' He tapped the tiny cassette recorder which he had attached to his lapel two hours earlier and spoken into at intervals. 'But I can recap the essentials for you easily enough, yes. The first fact indicates that it's hardly worth your hurrying: she's been dead for approximately two years.'

'How accurate is that?'

The doctor shrugged. 'In scientific terms, it's no more than an educated guess at the moment. We shall send some body tissue samples to the forensic laboratory at Chorley for further analysis. But if you're looking at the list of disappearances, I'd have to advise one to three years ago.'

Lucy Blake said, 'Dental records?'

'Ah! Much more promising. As you saw, the jaws are complete and undamaged.' He spoke with the enthusiasm of a man evaluating antique furniture. 'The forensic odontologist at the university will give you a dentistry profile that should produce reliable results; I'd say there is enough recent dental work for a positive match.'

Percy Peach said, 'And how old would she be when she was killed?'

'If you put me in court, I'd have to be cautious. Providing you don't quote me in that context, I'd say between seventeen and twenty-four. Again the forensic lab will be able to pinpoint it with further tests. But perhaps you'll have her identified by then.'

Peach looked at him suspiciously, wondering if he was being teased. He was not often a victim of such mistaken humour but you couldn't trust some of these professional men. 'Height and weight?'

'Height about 165 centimetres – about five feet six, in old money. Weight difficult to estimate, but she was young and reasonably fit. I'd say about nine stones, in normal circumstances.'

'Normal circumstances?' This was Lucy Blake, speaking quickly when she had meant to remain silent, half-suspecting already what was to come.

'She was pregnant. Three or four months, I'd say.' For the first time, the pathologist dropped his lightness of tone, no longer prepared to contend that this was no more than a job like any other, that the thing he had been working on was merely decaying refuse. The eyes of his listeners strayed for a moment to those sinister bowls with their black polythene covers, speculating despite themselves on which one of them might contain all that was left of that pathetic foetus.

It was Peach who said, 'Was she drowned?'

'No. She died by strangulation. There's no sign of a ligature, but the flesh at the throat and neck has almost totally gone. My guess would be manual strangulation. She was definitely dead when she went into the water, but at this distance it's impossible to tell how long before that she died.'

'Was she brought to the pond from a distance?'

'That again is impossible to say now. Had we had a cadaver in better condition, there would probably have been marks of carrying or transportation on it. All we can say is that heavy weights have been attached to the limbs. Presumably at the site where she was found.'

Peach nodded. 'She was weighted with rocks from around the quarry. Could she have been killed there?'

'She could indeed. But as I've explained, she could well have been killed a hundred miles away and brought there for disposal. I'm afraid there isn't enough of her left for us to help you with that.'

'Is there anything else you can tell us?'

'Only the obvious. Don't get the next of kin to do an identification, when you find out who they are. The dental records will be positive enough. As you've seen, we haven't much more than a skeleton with a few bits of damaged flesh under there.' He nodded towards the slabs where he had worked under their observation for most of the morning. 'There's no way I could sew that lot back together for examination by a relative.' He was back to his most robust, as if complaining about the inferior materials with which they had provided him.

While Peach was conferring with the exhibits officer about the rags of clothing which were to go to forensic, Lucy Blake slipped into the cloakroom. She looked in the mirror, happy to see that the blush make-up she had taken time to apply that morning was still doing its job. She had always had a strong stomach but there had been moments during the morning when it had been severely tested. She pressed her forehead for a moment against the cool of the mirror, then sipped a glass of cold water.

Then she took a deep breath and made for the door. As she went through it, she donned the bright confidence which she now regarded as her Percy Peach expression.

CHAPTER EIGHT

There are too many missing persons in modern Britain for any search among them to be easy. But the operators of the police computers had a time to start from: two years or thereabouts since this disappearance. And they had a place. They checked initially those women under twenty-six who had gone missing from homes within ten miles of Brunton.

Within two hours, they had a list of fourteen who seemed interesting candidates. It was entirely possible that this would be a false start, that the team would have to begin the lengthier sift through the National Home Office Missing Persons Register, established after bizarre discoveries of a positive graveyard of bodies of missing women at Cromwell Street, Gloucester, in 1994. But the searchers would try the obvious avenues before fanning outwards in the search.

In the first hours, the CID did not begin the interviewing of relatives. It was better to wait until they could be absolutely sure of the victim's identity. There was no point in causing further distress to parents and husbands who had already suffered years of alternating hope and despair. No point in starting false hares running; when three-quarters of all violent deaths are contrived within the family, the next of kin of a murder victim automatically become suspects, until such time as they can be eliminated.

After the well-publicized gaffes of the last decade, the public are nowadays suspicious of the police, sensitive about any false starts, only too happy to accuse officers of bumbling indifference, even when known criminals are pulled in for questioning. Therefore there is an even greater need to

be sure of your facts when you are beginning a murder
investigation which has already had the publicity of a melodramatic discovery of the corpse.

Superintendent Tucker was well aware of all this. Whatever Peach and others thought of him as a policeman, he
had studied his public relations techniques. In his press
conferences, he exuded a businesslike determination. For
Granada Television, he promised, with full confidence, that
they would 'get to the bottom of this one', that 'no stone
would be left unturned in the search for the person responsible for this callous disposal of a young woman in the
prime of life'. With his mastery of the telling cliché thus
established, he assured the camera earnestly that 'the public
had his personal guarantee' that the dead girl would soon be
identified.

He had every reason for confidence in this last assertion.
An hour before he made it, the dental records had provided
them with conclusive proof of the identity of the remains
which had been immersed for so long. By the end of the
day, the parents would have been informed and the name
would be released to the media. Superintendent Tucker's
first promise would be vindicated. The public would have
the confidence of a sound man in charge of the investigation, a man who was already producing results. No one,
Tucker liked to think, managed the release of information
more tellingly than he did.

The forensic odontologists confirmed that the woman
was one of the fourteen thrown up by the initial computer
search in the Brunton nick. The one, in fact, who had lived
nearest to the point on the North Lancs golf course where
the corpse had been found. A woman without any previous
police record, whether as criminal or victim.

That evening, Superintendent Tucker was able to reveal
that the victim was a girl called Debbie Minton.

Tucker had passed the information to Peach within sixty

seconds of receiving it. His air was that of a man who had done the hard work and was now generously turning the routine conclusion of a case over to his grateful underlings. He put down the internal phone, fiddled with the buttons on his desk until he was satisfied that the light outside illuminated the 'Engaged' disc, and retrieved a putter from the regulation steel issue wardrobe in the corner of the big office. An executive deserved some reward for his efforts.

Two floors below him, Percy Peach studied the words he had scribbled down on the pad as he listened to Tommy Bloody Tucker's lordly release of the information. So the investigation proper could now commence, and the foot soldiers could get on with it. He glared at his ball-penned phrases, as if by sheer concentration he could develop some detail around the bald facts of the girl's identity and age.

Peach knew, as Tucker knew but had not cared to acknowledge, that they must now begin to build up a picture of the dead woman. Murder is one of the few crimes where the victim cannot speak for herself, cannot give her own version of the criminal act which has sparked an investigation. Her personality, her sexual inclinations, her prejudices, above all the way she has lived, are the most important indications of who has killed her. Yet these things must be built up through the mouths of others, through accounts which often conflict, and which come from people who have their own reasons to conceal parts of the truth.

And this victim had been dead and undiscovered for two years. There was the added dimension of time to complicate the normal obscurities for those attempting to assemble the picture of the victim.

Peach pondered these things, then snapped at Lucy Blake, 'First job is to tell the parents. You'd best get round there and break it to the mother.'

His sergeant looked at him steadily from beneath the dark red hair. 'Tea and sympathy, is it, sir? The woman's role? Arm round the poor creature's shoulders, whilst the men get on with the investigation? It's a job that needs doing, certainly. I suggest we get a uniformed WPC to go round there right away, whilst we get on with some detection.'

'Don't order me about, Sergeant Blake. I'll decide who does what round here. And if you don't like it, you know – '

'I didn't order anyone about, Sir. It was a suggestion. At most a reminder of what I'm supposed to be here for. Sir.'

Peach noticed how white his spotless knuckles were on the edge of the desk in front of him. Why did this woman rile him so much more than any of the criminal riff-raff he dealt with so readily? Wasn't she supposed to be on the same side as him, for God's sake? He snapped, 'Oh, for Christ's sake stop the bloody "Sirs", can't you? At least when we're alone.'

He was the more enraged because he knew he had seen her in just the role she had rejected, comforting the afflicted mother whilst he got on with digging for the facts. Well, women were supposed to be good at that, weren't they? So why did this woman have to be so damned touchy? So unfeminine? She didn't look like a dyke to him. She didn't even smell like one, he thought for the first time, becoming aware of a light perfume which his small office had probably never encountered until today. But then he had not the vaguest idea of how lesbians were supposed to smell.

She stood not five feet from him, awaiting orders, her face unsmiling, save for the ghost of amusement he thought he detected in her green eyes. He allowed himself the heavy sigh of the exploited but eternally patient male. Then he said, 'We'll go to the Mintons' house together. See what gives. Play it by ear. Watch their reactions to the news. You'll probably end up comforting the poor woman though, like I said.'

Neither of them had any illusion that Percy Peach had saved face.

The pleasant semi-detached house looked much like the

others in the road. It had a neat front garden where roses still flowered profusely, as if by their activity they could delay the autumn and prolong the Indian summer which yet hung bright over Lancashire.

Lucy Blake was still young enough for death to be something of a novelty. It still seemed wrong to her that violent death could have such an ordinary setting, that its horror should not be marked by some livid mark upon the victim's house, which would set the place apart and warn those who came here on routine business to wrap the tragic occupants in metaphorical cotton wool, until their scars were healed enough to be displayed to the world at large.

The lawn was cut and edged: there was not a weed to be seen. The tidiness was almost obsessive. But then there was a reason for obsession, if that was what this indicated: this house had lost a daughter two years ago. It was only the final sentence, the line that drew finis at the end of a life, that was to be announced today.

It was Derek Minton who opened the door to them, and their trained, observant eyes saw immediately that the house was as tidy inside as out. Nothing was out of place. The spotless kitchen they glimpsed through the door from the hall might never have seen a meal prepared. In the living room where Minton led them, even the day's newspaper was folded neatly within the brass magazine holder, as if it had never been opened. The curtains were held in their swatches, each fold answered by a matching fold at the other side of the window. And the woman who sat upright in the armchair and looked at the empty fireplace was still as a statue.

Minton said, 'They gave me the day off. Compassionate grounds, you see.' He smiled at them nervously. They could see in his eyes that he knew.

Peach said awkwardly, 'I think it would be better if you sat down for a minute, Mr Minton.' He knew he was not good at this sort of thing. For a moment, he wished that he had let the uniformed branch handle the breaking of this news. But he had the instincts of a hunter, and experience as well as statistics told him that those closest to a murder victim were often involved in the death, even if not directly. He needed to study the reactions of these parents.

Derek Minton said, 'It's Debbie, isn't it? We heard about the body being found, you see.'

With the mention of the name, the woman in the armchair turned to acknowledge them, showing no surprise, though previously she had given no sign that she had even been conscious of their entry into her house. Perhaps she hoped that they would be able to deny what her husband had said. But there was no real hope in her face.

Lucy Blake went and knelt beside her, taking the listless hands into her more active ones, surprised to find them warm where she had expected a marble cold. She nodded at Shirley Minton, feeling the tears starting to her own eyes, holding them back because she knew they would not help. Behind her, Percy Peach said, 'I'm afraid it is Debbie, yes, Mr Minton. We've had the report in from the forensic people. I'm sorry, but there's no room for doubt.'

There was a small movement in the hands which Blake held tightly. But no wild sobbing. No screaming that this could not be so. Not a tear, as yet. Shirley Minton said quietly, 'Can I see her?'

For the first time since she had met him, Lucy was glad to hear the inspector's voice. It was firm but a little husky as he said, 'That wouldn't be wise, Mrs Minton. It will be better to remember her as you knew her. That's the real Debbie, you see.'

The mother nodded, accepting the advice as meekly as if she had been guided on a choice of dress for a function. 'She'll be damaged, I suppose, after all that time in the water.'

Lucy nodded, grateful for this acceptance, fearful that if she spoke she might break the fragile acquiescence. When there was no word from either of the men behind her, she said, 'You'll be able to have a proper funeral, of course, and mourn her as you would want to. It – it's awful news for us to bring to you, I know. But you and Debbie's dad will have to comfort each other. At least after all this time you know for certain. Now you can begin to grieve for your daughter . . .'

She was aware that she was talking too much, trying to find a way out of the emotional cul-de-sac into which she had led herself. It was a relief when the woman smiled down at her and said unexpectedly, 'Derek isn't her father you know. Her dad's dead.'

Behind her, Lucy heard Derek Minton's voice say nervously, 'But I've been around a long time now, you know, love. Since Charlie was eleven and Debbie was nine. They were like my own children to me.'

'He was always good to them.' Shirley looked straight into Lucy's wide green eyes, as if it was necessary for her to convince her of that, to defend her husband. 'And he's been a good man to me, has Derek. We'll be all right, I expect, now we know.' She nodded, as if considering the proposition for the first time and approving it. Then she looked back into the concerned young face of the woman who knelt beside her. 'You're not much older than our Debbie, lass. Did you know her?'

'No, I didn't, Mrs Minton. I've only just been posted here, you see. From over Garstang way.' She dropped into the Lancashire accent she had striven to lose, straining for closeness with the woman in shock beside her. Shirley Minton was about the same age as her own mother, whom she had been so happy to leave as she struck out into the world on her own, so glad to return to in times of stress. 'But we shall be talking to lots of people who did know her. You'll be able to help us there, I expect. Give us some names.'

'When shall us bury her, Derek?' Shirley's own Lancashire came out strong as she spoke directly to her husband, for the first time since they had come into the house.

Minton hesitated, looking at Peach, knowing what was coming. The inspector said, 'There'll have to be an inquest. But the coroner will open it in a couple of days' time. That will only be a five-minute job, and there won't be any need for you to be there: we can give the evidence of identification. I'm sure the coroner will be prepared to issue a death certificate and a burial order, so that you can make funeral arrangements.'

Minton said, 'You must find out who killed her for us.' But he spoke without real passion, as if this was a sentiment he had rehearsed because he knew it would be required of him.

Peach noted automatically that Minton had accepted without needing to be convinced that this was murder. That was not significant; the press reports of the corpse at the bottom of the quarry pit had all suggested foul play, and Tucker had already admitted as much as he courted the television publicity. He said, 'We shall find the person or persons responsible, Mr Minton. You can be assured of that.'

He looked from the man beside him to the woman in the chair. 'We shall need your help with that. Not today, of course, but as soon as you feel that you can – '

'She left here at eight o'clock on October the twentieth. That will be two years ago, in nine days' time. We haven't heard a word from her since that day.' She spoke evenly, like one in a dream. For the first time, the visitors had a vivid glimpse of what this couple had been through in those two years.

Derek Minton said, 'I'm going to be off work for a couple of days. Perhaps I could come and see you tomorrow, and answer whatever questions you would like to put to me.'

His wife looked up at him, offering the first smile that any one of the four had given since this had begun. 'He likes to shield me, you know, when he can. But I shall be here, when you want me. I expect you'll want the names of her friends. She was a good girl, you know, Debbie. Lively, yes, but always a good girl to us.' Suddenly, she was weeping, clasping the policewoman to her, as she would never clasp again the daughter she had loved.

In the car outside, Lucy Blake said, 'I'm glad that's over.'

It was her first admission of any sort of weakness to him. He said, 'It's never much fun, that sort of thing. I've known much worse. I thought we did well, really.'

They rode back to the station in silence. She was surprised to find that she rather liked that 'we'.

CHAPTER NINE

Because Tommy Tucker rarely moved out of the new block which was the Brunton Police headquarters, the resources which formed the back-up to a murder inquiry were readily available.

Tucker might be held in contempt by working coppers, but human nature operates as predictably in the police force as in any other large organization. He carried the rank, so people were careful not to offend him. Indeed, while Percy Peach was a notable and admired exception, most people took pains to please Tucker. The man might be a prat, but he was a prat who controlled careers, and the men and women involved recognized it.

Because Tucker was always around, because he was better at checking the easy things like furniture and photography than how his staff were conducting themselves in the public world outside, the Murder Room assembled to pursue the killers of Debbie Minton was most impressive. Computers and operators; filing cabinets and a filing clerk; tables, chairs, trays; a blackboard and a plaster board with photographs of the remains at the shattered old quarry; large-scale maps of Brunton and the North Lancashire golf course; three extra telephones and an overhead projector.

It was all very impressive, as were the rotas of officers and the residences they had to cover on the house-to-house inquiries. Personnel are expensive, and there are never enough of them. But on a murder inquiry, the stops are pulled out and there are not the normal queries from on high about exceeding the overtime hours allotted in the budget.

This energy was all very well, thought Percy Peach, except that the girl had been dead for two years. Piecing together her last hours, the normal first objective in any murder search, was going to be almost impossible. Tommy Bloody Tucker had everything set up impeccably, but was all this equipment going to lead them anywhere?

As if to confirm his doubts, the phone on his desk shrilled with the latest news from forensic. The pathetic remains of the foetus which had reposed within the water-damaged body would yield no information beyond the bare fact that Debbie Minton had been about three months pregnant. Neither a blood group nor a DNA profile could be extracted for possible matching with any possible father. If they were going to find this father, the man who might well have dispatched this unfortunate mother-to-be, it would have to be by detective work alone.

He went back to his office to wait for Derek Minton.

In the spotlessly tidy semi-detached house on the outskirts of Brunton, Lucy Blake studied Shirley Minton, watching for any reaction to the sound of the soft footsteps above their heads.

The grieving mother had raised no objection to the search of her daughter's room, seeming scarcely to hear the carefully worded explanation of the clues it might offer to her daughter's movements and companions in the weeks before her death. Nevertheless, Lucy had thought it politic to stay with her in the comfortable lounge, whilst the man and woman in uniform went about their task in the tidy room upstairs.

There was no knowing, of course, how much the parents had already removed, wittingly or unwittingly, which might have been of value. Debbie Minton had been nineteen and a half when she disappeared: few girls of that age kept their rooms as clinically neat as the one they had been ushered into upstairs.

As if she had caught that thought, Shirley Minton said suddenly, 'I tidied the place up, when she didn't come back that first weekend. No one has slept in there since, of course. It was waiting for her to come back.'

The police saw it often enough when they went into people's houses. The room preserved as a shrine to the youngster who had disappeared, even when he or she had died in a road accident and the parents knew from the start that they could never be back. You tried sometimes to talk them away from it, as if you were a medic or a social worker. Usually they said, 'It's all we have left, you see,' as if that were all the explanation that was needed. It might be morbid, but there was a kind of logic in it. And those who had never experienced such losses should not push the sufferers too hard. WDS Blake, sitting watchfully attentive on the edge of her chair, knew by now that the worst thing that you could say was that you understood.

Lucy said, 'You haven't taken anything away from the room, that you can remember? It's surprising what can be useful to us, you see. We don't always know ourselves what is going to be significant, at first.'

Shirley Minton shook her head, her brown eyes as earnest as a child's. 'No. I've thought about that. I washed a few of her clothes, that she'd worn earlier in the week. The other things I just tidied away into the drawers. There wasn't a lot. A few CDs and tapes. She didn't have a library book up there. There were a couple of paperbacks on the floor by the bed, but I just put those on the shelves.'

'I suppose you washed the sheets that were on the bed.'

A little start. 'Yes. I suppose I should have told you about that. Does it matter?'

'No, of course not. It was a natural thing to do,' said Lucy hastily. But there could be no tests now for semen, no suggestive fibres from clothing which did not belong to the dead girl. She was beginning to appreciate Peach's complaints about the scent being cold.

'She was a good girl, you know. Always a good daughter. Never forgot my birthday, nor Derek's. We didn't bother much with things like Mother's Day. American invention, we thought.' Mrs Minton studied the backs of her hands as if there might be a clue there to these inexplicable events.

Lucy left her for a moment, looking out over the trim lawn to where a spray chrysanthemum glowed like new gold against the evergreens. She fed her questions in whenever an opening offered itself; your timing had to be subtle with the bereaved. 'Did she have many boyfriends?'

'No. I don't think she ever brought one home. She was a lively girl, mind, but I think she liked to be in a crowd. She went to the youth club a lot, round at St Margaret's. Leastways, she did when she was younger, and I think the same crowd went around together, even after they felt they'd grown out of table tennis and Coke.' She smiled over the last phrase, and Lucy knew suddenly that it had come from the dead girl herself.

'She worked as a typist, I believe?'

'At Postlethwaites' yes. The furnishers in the centre of town. She hadn't been there long but she was doing quite well. Apparently there was the chance of her becoming a secretary to one of the bosses. Only they don't call it that now, apparently. A personal helper or something.'

'Personal assistant, yes. She was doing well, then. Were there people from work that she associated with? In the evenings or at the weekends, I mean.' There was one at least who would need to be checked out: the one who had chosen to promote this so far unremarkable girl to be his PA. If, of course, that was more than a fond mother's illusion.

In the room upstairs, the two methodical searchers were finding some surprising material. Things that did not altogether confirm the mother's picture of her daughter.

In the room below them, Lucy Blake said quietly, 'Can you remember exactly what time Debbie went out on that last night, Mrs Minton?'

'It was about eight o'clock, I believe. I had a job myself in those days, on the check-out at Tesco's. Friday was our late night, so I was out, but Derek said she went out at about eight. That was about her usual time.' She had been over all this before in her own mind, many times. The phrases tumbled out ready-made.

'And she never said whom she was intending to see?'

'No. The usual crowd, we think. They asked us all about it when she was registered as a missing person.'

'Yes, I know. But you'll understand that we don't want to miss anything. Of course, Debbie might not have died that night. It might have been weeks later. She might have been with someone that you never even knew. Perhaps someone who didn't even come from round here.'

Shirley Minton's brown eyes opened wide, even as her forehead wrinkled with this new thought. 'But she was found near here, wasn't she? Not much more than a mile away from home.'

She had put her finger on one of the key facts. Lucy agreed that that seemed to indicate a local killer, but that they must be alive to all the possibilities. She heard the two uniformed officers coming down the stairs, moving slowly, with the two boxes they were going to take to the Murder Room held awkwardly before them.

Shirley Minton looked suddenly near to panic, as if she was about to query the removal of these secret things. Lucy moved quickly to the sideboard. 'This is a lovely picture of Debbie,' she said, picking up the photograph Shirley had dusted so longingly for two years. 'May I take it with me to get copies made for our team to carry?' Then, as she saw consternation surging into the mother's pale face, she added hastily, 'It will help to prod people's memories around the town, you see. And I can have it back to you by the end of the day.'

Shirley Minton took it from her for a moment, looking lovingly down into the wide brown eyes which were like younger versions of her own. Then she thrust it into Lucy's hands. 'Take good care of her, won't you love? She's all I've got left, now.'

So that phrase had come out in the end, after all. Lucy carried the photograph out to the panda car as carefully as if it had been a live thing, trying not to notice the mother's eyes which followed her movements from the other side of the glass.

Percy Peach was tempted to take Derek Minton into an interview room. These were Percy's natural metier. There was no escape from his dark eyes in those claustrophobic cells, with their basic furniture of small square table and two or three upright chairs. No movement that would not be seen, no word that would not be heard. The bright day outside would be firmly excluded by those windowless walls.

It was tempting, but it was too early yet for that. If, later, Derek Minton proved to be a suspect; if he even seemed to be holding anything back from them . . .

Percy saw him in his own office, coming forward affably to shake his hand, seating him carefully in the best arm-chair, thanking him for coming in so readily to help them in these distressing circumstances. Then he began to probe. The cruel step-parent of fairy tales may be an unfair concept to foist upon children, now that so many of them have to contend with one in real life. But policemen see enough evil things in that same real life to make stepfathers in particular interesting figures.

Percy gave his visitor a mug of police tea. There were those with sensitive taste buds who would have said that was an opening gesture of hostility, but he did not intend it to be so. When each of them was cradling a steaming beaker, he said, 'How many years is it since you married your wife, Mr Minton?'

'Twelve. Twelve and a half I suppose, now. Shirley was a widow, and I'd divorced my first wife before I met her.'

'Which was how long before you married?'

'Two years. Shirley's first husband had only been dead for eight months when we first met. She came into the old council offices to ask about help with her rates. I was on the counter then.' He took a sip of his tea, smiling for a moment at the memory. He was not as tall as Peach had thought him at first; about five feet ten, he now decided. He looked taller because he was slim and wiry. He crossed his thin legs and kept his grey, watchful eyes on the inspector's face.

Peach said, 'No doubt it wasn't easy, taking on the children at that age.'

Minton paused for a moment, then shrugged. 'Charlie was eleven and Debbie was nine. There were a few problems at first, but only what you'd expect. They'd been quite attached to their father, and don't forget he'd died, not walked out on them. Charlie was a bit difficult, and that carried on through adolescence. I don't think there was ever a problem with Debbie.'

Peach said, 'It's early days, Mr Minton. But so far, you're the last person we know who saw Debbie alive.' It wasn't Percy's way to wrap these things up. You often got a better reaction if you didn't.

Minton was not put out. He leaned forward, as if he was glad to be getting down to the business of the investigation after the opening exchanges. 'I've been over it a hundred times, as you can imagine. It was a Friday night. Late in October – Shirley could give you the actual date. Debbie went out at about eight o'clock.'

Peach paused, studying the lean, earnest face opposite him. 'You got on well with your daughter, Mr Minton?'

'I got on very well with her. Forgive me, but would it be any of your business if I hadn't done?'

Peach smiled. He had no wish to upset this man – there was nothing against him yet. But nor would he give him an easy ride. 'It would be very much my business, as a matter of fact. This is a murder investigation, sir. Someone brutally killed your stepdaughter – or your daughter, if you prefer to regard her as that.'

'I do. I've been around since she was nine, you know. And she'd taken my name. As far as I'm concerned, she's my daughter.'

'Right. Good. That means you'll be anxious to give us every co-operation in building up the fullest possible picture of your daughter.' Peach made it sound as if that had not been the man's intention, as if he had won a victory and would now conduct the interview on his terms.

Derek Minton felt it too; he was not quite sure how the situation had come about. He said defensively, 'What is it you want to know?'

'Everything you can remember. The fuller the picture we can build up of the last months of Debbie's life, the better our chances of determining who killed her.'

'Isn't it possible that her killer was someone she didn't even know? Someone she met for the first time on the night she died? Someone who didn't even come from this area?'

'It's entirely possible.' Peach gave him a grim little smile. 'Speaking as a detective, I hope it isn't. We've a much better chance of an early arrest if the person responsible for her death knew her well and is still in the area.'

Minton nodded miserably. 'I suppose that's right.' He looked down at his feet, whilst Percy wondered if this was really the first time that thought had entered his mind. 'This is going to be a desperate business.'

Peach, controlling an unexpected surge of sympathy, said briskly, 'It is indeed. But the more co-operation we get, the sooner we'll have a result and be able to lay your daughter's memory decently to rest. Let's start with a list of the people she knew. I'd like the name of anyone with whom she was in regular contact in the months before her death. Every contact, even the one which seems most innocent, is of interest at this stage. You mustn't think we're looking for suspects: we're just getting a picture of the friends and the movements of a young woman whom none of us knows.'

Minton looked troubled, even a little sullen. 'I can't remember all of them, at this distance in time.'

'Of course not. But we shall be talking to a lot of people in the next few days. Spreading the net wider and wider, unless something suggestive turns up quickly. If you forget anyone, we shall collect the name from someone else.' Might as well let him know that to start with. Best to discourage his memory from any attempt at selection.

Minton was looking thoroughly uncomfortable. Perhaps he had expected a more sympathetic atmosphere, like the one at the house yesterday. Peach, studiously failing to notice his discomfort, was riding on it, even enjoying it. Percy liked murder inquiries; they gave him the excuse to tread upon a few corns. Minton looked down into his half-empty mug of tea, as if he had forgotten it was there, then finished it carefully, though it must have been cold. Perhaps he was stealing a little time to gather his thoughts. Eventually he said, 'You'll be talking to Shirley?'

'We have to, I'm afraid. Detective Sergeant Blake is probably there at this moment, as a matter of fact. Obviously we'll be as gentle as possible. And as I explained yesterday, we'll need to have a detailed look at your daughter's room.'

Minton nodded. 'Shirley's been better, since Debbie was found, strangely enough. She's determined we'll get her killer.' He looked bleakly into his empty cup, as though the prospect of the hunt depressed him.

Peach was a little puzzled by that. According to what he'd heard in the last twenty-four hours, Shirley Minton had been a handful for her husband in the last two years: the thought of having the whole business cleared up should gladden him. Percy said cheerfully, 'I'm glad to hear that "we". If we all work together, with your knowledge and our resources, there's every chance we'll get the person responsible quite quickly.'

Minton had not looked at him for some time. He was still looking at his toe-caps as he said, 'You may not get the same picture from Shirley as from other people, you know.'

Peach knew that a mother's view of her daughter was rarely the same as the rest of the world's. But he did not volunteer that comforting assurance to the man in the armchair. Let him work out his own solution to the problem he had set himself. What Percy in fact said was, 'You'd better enlarge on that for me, Mr Minton.'

The man still did not look up. Instead, he muttered, 'Debbie was nineteen and a half when she left. She was a lively girl. Not the saint her mother will tell you she was.'

Peach said, 'You won't shock me, Mr Minton. Whatever she was like, you can be assured that we have seen very much worse.'

It was harsh comfort, but it was the first encouragement Minton had been given, and he was grateful for it. 'She – she enjoyed herself . . .' He stopped and looked up at Peach, opening his palms in a little gesture of supplication.

'Drugs?'

Minton shrugged. 'I don't know. Sometimes I thought so, but I could never be certain. I'm sure she never brought them into the house.'

Peach wondered how many parents really knew what their daughters did these days. Very few, in his experience; he was glad that he had been spared children. 'Drink?'

'Sometimes. It doesn't take much to get young girls drunk, does it?'

'Did she come home drunk?'

'No. Never. I don't think she could have faced Shirley in that condition. But she was very late home, sometimes. And I felt she might have behaved stupidly outside the house as a result of drink.'

'Stupidly. With men?'

Minton actually looked relieved rather than outraged. 'There were men, yes.'

'A lot of men?'

'I – I couldn't say. I heard people talking, sometimes.'

'Boys of her own age? Older men?'

This time Minton did look upset. 'Mostly boys of her own age. But I think there were one or two older men as well. I questioned her about it but she either laughed it off or just clammed up.'

'She didn't deny it?'

'No, just refused to talk about it.'

Peach stopped the questioning, waiting for the man to look up at him, knowing that it would happen if he only waited long enough. When Derek Minton's troubled blue eyes were eventually drawn up to meet his, he said curtly, 'Forgive the question: you're intelligent enough to know why it has to be asked. Would you say that your daughter was promiscuous, Mr Minton?'

The man in the armchair winced at the word. But he did not yell his pain, screaming the agony which was the more acute because he knew it was the truth, as Peach had seen in parents and husbands often enough to be ready to deal with it. Instead, Minton's shoulders dropped a little at each side of the slim head and he said, 'I'm not sure I know what the word means, technically. But I suppose she was, yes. I think she had sex with several different men in the year before she died, so I suppose that's promiscuity.'

He was very calm. His delivery of the phrases was almost clinical. Perhaps he had considered the question in the quiet hours of the night, as the weeks of the girl's disappearance had stretched into months and the months into years. Peach said quietly, 'We shall need a list from you of who you think these partners were.'

'I can't give you all of them. Some of it would only be surmise. I told you, she didn't talk to me about – '

'That's all right, Mr Minton. Just tell us the names of all the people that you know were in contact with Debbie in the months before she left. We'll do our own investigations into how close those relationships were.'

The blue eyes were cast steadily upon the carpet again. The mouth set into a sullen line. 'I doubt whether I'll be able to help you.'

A bit of resistance. Far more in Percy Peach's line than treading carefully with bereaved relatives. He licked his lips like an eager terrier. 'You seem more anxious to protect these people than to find out who killed your daughter, Mr Minton. I find that curious, to say the least.'

He was delighted to see the shock in the blue eyes as they flashed up at him. Derek Minton said, 'Of course I'm desperate that you should find out who killed Debbie. But I don't want anyone falsely accused, do I?'

Peach found the usual roles curiously reversed. The bereaved parent who should have been baying emotionally for blood was counselling the caution and fairness which should have come from the CID man, exercising the objective, dispassionate view. He did not trouble to answer the man's rhetorical question. Instead, he said after a moment's pause, 'Did you know that Debbie was pregnant, Mr Minton?'

Shock; anger; a reluctant acceptance. Peach watched the emotions that should be there flashing in rapid, overlapping succession across the man's face. Minton's shoulders gave a shrug which was probably unconscious, which would certainly have passed unnoticed by anyone scrutinizing the man less acutely than the inspector. He said in a voice which was only just audible, 'I didn't know that.'

'Have you any suggestion as to who the father might have been?'

'No. I told you. There were quite a lot of young men around her. Any one of them might have . . . Will I need to tell Shirley about this?'

'Someone will have to, I'm afraid. It will come out, you see. Quickly; probably when the inquest is opened.'

Minton thought for a moment, then nodded, wretched but resigned. 'I'll tell her. It will come better from me than from anyone else.' He seemed to find a bleak consolation in that.

He gave Peach some names, which would be added to the growing list on the computer in the Murder Room outside, cross-referenced with those coming in from other sources. Percy made him understand that any information he held back would emerge from elsewhere; that any such omissions on his part would then become interesting to the investigating team. As far as he could judge, Minton was co-operative and anxious only to help the hunt.

It was when he had gone that the sergeant who had been sifting the contents of the boxes brought in from Debbie Minton's room came into Peach's office. He had the mournful look and heavy jowls of a bloodhound, and a pessimistic temperament which might have been chosen to match them. 'Very little that looks significant,' he said glumly. 'You wouldn't expect it, after two years. The parents must have been over that room with a toothcomb.'

'No pictures of boyfriends? No diaries?'

'Nothing like that,' said Sergeant Etherington, with what sounded almost like satisfaction. 'Forensic may come up with something, but it's my guess that there isn't a fibre in there that doesn't come from the clothes in the girl's wardrobe.'

'According to her father, she didn't entertain her admirers at home, anyway,' said Peach.

Etherington had one tiny thing to offer. He produced it like a miser releasing treasure. 'We did find something. It may not mean anything.' Like all people of his temperament, he tried to anticipate disappointment by dampening expectations.

'Well? I haven't got all day.'

Etherington produced a paperback thriller with a lurid cover. He put the book on the desk in front of Peach and turned to the inside of the back cover. Six figures were written close together there, so neatly that they almost seemed part of the brief biography of the author printed above them.

A phone number, perhaps. There was no code, so probably a local one: Peach recognized the first two numbers, which seemed to confirm that idea. 'Have you checked it out?'

'Yes.' Etherington permitted himself a tiny smile at his efficiency. 'It's the number of the hospital which does abortions.' His face resumed its normal dismal cast. 'They have no record of a contact from the girl or anyone acting on her behalf.'

Peach glared for ten seconds at the neat set of numbers with his characteristic intensity, as if the fierceness of his concentration would make them yield up their secret. 'Is it the girl's own writing?'

Etherington was gratified by the question: the corners of his mouth straightened for a moment. 'We'll ask forensic to get their graphologist on it in due course. It's a pity there's no writing with it. But we do have an exercise book with a few figures from the dead girl in it. I would be confident that she didn't write that number down herself.'

The two men looked in silence at the neat series of upright numbers. Both of them knew it was possible they had been written by the murderer of Debbie Minton.

CHAPTER TEN

Percy Peach admitted to a certain prejudice against vicars. He would have put it down to an unfortunate childhood experience, had he not rejected that explanation so often from criminals and their tame psyches.

He took Lucy Blake with him to see the Reverend Joseph Jackson, in case he needed to be kept in check. It would at least provide his new detective sergeant with some sort of function, when he could see bugger-all else for her to do. He would have taken DS Collins with him in the old days and the new woman seemed to think she had the right to assume all the side-kick duties that that long streak of discretion had fulfilled. It was strange how last week had so quickly become 'the old days'. Viewed through the tinted glasses of a rapidly growing nostalgia, Collins had begun to seem quite a good bloke. At least he had known when to keep his mouth shut.

Joseph Jackson turned out to be one of the newer breed of clergy, all social awareness and guitars and none of your dogma and solemn services. 'Do call me Joe, everyone does!' he said, as he pumped the police hands vigorously in turn. Percy immediately became conscious of a need he had never perceived before in the church for formality and ritual. Even a touch of incense might not come amiss, he felt. There should be required a certain dignified remoteness in the representatives of God on earth. If they did not carry this, they merited the robust treatment Percy accorded to most of their flocks.

'We're here about this dead girl. Debbie Minton. Parishioner of yours and good-time girl, until someone decided to put an end to her.'

Even the vicar's professional cheerfulness was clouded for a moment by this uncompromising beginning. He had a fresh and rosy face, eyebrows which seemed perpetually about to take flight like doves from the ecclesiastical brow, large white teeth which might have been designed for display in his habitual smile. He was thirty-six and had been the holder of his post here for six years now; those two facts Percy had been able to check before he came to beard him in his vicarage.

It was a high-roomed Victorian vicarage, but the church had compromised with slender modern revenues by dividing it into two. A parishioner with an eye for potential had purchased the other and sunnier half of the building, then sold it within three years at a handsome profit to an ungodly academic. This man had announced cheerfully that he was conducting an objective study of the present incumbent's declining congregation and workload.

Joe Jackson had glanced nervously over the fence towards his invisible neighbour when the police car drew up outside. He tried not to speculate about the man's researches as he addressed himself to Peach's inquiries about Debbie Minton. He was faced with a situation he met often nowadays. It was unfair to claim the girl had been a regular attender at his services, but a denial might cause offence to the relatives. But this was official. He had decided before these people came that he had better be as straightforward as he dared. That had to be the right approach, so long as he took care to conceal the one vital fact that could be disastrous.

Yet he found it difficult to speak. He did not like the look of this barrel of energy with the fringe of black hair round the shining bald pate. With his small white teeth and his lip slipping into the gaps where the upper canines were missing, DI Peach looked like a beaver preparing to gnaw at the dam of a man's resistance.

The Reverend Joseph Jackson eventually managed to say, 'I – I think it would be stretching things to say she was a regular parishioner. She used to come fairly often to the youth club, in the old days, I suppose.'

'And how often is fairly often?' Peach rapped out his first question as if he had already spotted a weakness in an adversary.

'Well, I suppose you could say she was a regular attender, in the days when she came.'

'Twice a week? Three times a week? Every night?' The small white teeth flashed briefly from the flat, aggressive face. The larger teeth opposite him were now hardly on display at all.

Jackson licked dry lips. 'The club is open five nights a week. I suppose Debbie Minton used to be there on most of those, in the period we're speaking about.'

'We haven't spoken about any period yet, Joseph. Are you saying that she'd ceased to be a regular attender in the months before she died?'

'But I don't know when she died, do I?' He managed a weak grin to accompany this challenge: at least he had not fallen for that one. But it showed the need for perpetual vigilance; it must be the business of people like this to trip up inexperienced people like him.

'Really? Well, the scientists seem pretty convinced that she died about two years ago. Or was brutally murdered, if you haven't picked up that detail either.' Peach gave him his full killer shark grin, as if in mockery of the nervous gesture towards mirth Jackson had just produced. 'Debbie Minton disappeared exactly two years ago, as even you must be aware, Vicar. How long before that did you last see her?'

Jackson was not sure when a visit to find out the facts about Debbie Minton's social habits had turned into a personal interrogation, but he had no time to dwell on the puzzle. 'I – I couldn't be sure of that. I don't think I had much contact at all with her in that last year. She'd stopped coming to the youth club, of course. They mostly do, when they feel themselves older than the youngsters coming in. It's a great pity in my view that – '

'When did she stop coming to the youth club?'

'When she was about seventeen and a half, I think. They mostly stop about then. Begin to think they're adults. They're not, of course, but – '

'Two years before she disappeared, then. Four years ago from now?'

'Yes.'

'But you just said you'd seen her in the year before she died.'

'Did I?' He sought furiously through a brain that was too excited to work properly for the memory of what he had said no more than a minute earlier. 'No, I think you'll find – '

'I asked you when you last saw her and you said you did not have much contact with her in that last year. "Not much" means some, in my book. So you saw her at least once. Unless you're now changing your story.' He liked that word. When vicars had talked of telling stories when he was a lad in short trousers, they had always meant lies.

'It's a long time ago now. I must have seen her in the year before she disappeared, if only about the town. I can't re-member seeing her at a church service, I'm afraid. It might have been better for her if she had kept up her church attendance. But then you could say I have an axe to grind there, couldn't you?' Aware that he was now saying too much, he broke off with an involuntary giggle, high-pitched and weird, which seemed to reverberate away into the high corners above the Victorian frieze. Peach regarded him impassively, like a powerful cat waiting to pounce on its prey's first clumsy move.

Jackson turned in desperation to look at the female detect-ive sergeant, hoping for a softer response from her. Instead,

Lucy Blake said, 'Mrs Minton seemed to think that she was still attending the youth club, right up to the time of her disappearance. Would you care to comment on that, Mr Jackson?' There was a smile on the lightly freckled face beneath the red hair, but she made it sound as if the discrepancy in the accounts of the girl made his story suspect, just as her awful boss had done.

Joe Jackson wondered if that was something they taught them at the police school, if they had such things. He swallowed hard, finding to his surprise that it took him two attempts to do so. 'She stopped coming to the club when she was seventeen and a half. More than two years before she disappeared.'

Lucy Blake's head moved fractionally to one side. Perhaps she was surprised that he should suddenly be so certain of the timing, but she said nothing. Jackson fingered his dog collar briefly, as if he wished to make sure that it was still in place. Then he said, 'Perhaps she gave her mother to understand that she was still coming here when she was going off to other, less salubrious places. It happens, I'm afraid.'

Percy Peach had already decided from his conversation with Derek Minton that his daughter had done just that. But he saw no reason to let this sky pilot off the hook to which he had so obligingly attached himself. 'What was your own relationship with Debbie Minton, Mr Jackson?'

He found the effect of this most gratifying. The vicar's jaw dropped for a moment and his blue eyes opened wide. Though he swiftly corrected these things, he could not disguise the way the colour drained from his high cheeks: his countryman's redness of countenance did not permit deception here. He said, 'I was friendly with her, as I was with all of the young people in our youth club. No more than that.'

'Nothing – what's the right word now – improper? But you must have got to know her quite well, in those impressionable years when she came here five nights a week. How close to her did you get?' Percy liked that deliberately clumsy, deliberately ambiguous phrase. No one could take exception to it, but it carried a hint of the unsavoury.

'I – I helped her as best I could through the trials of adolescence. That is no more and no less than it was my duty to do as a minister of the Church.' Joe rarely invoked his cloth as a defence; he wondered if it now rang as defensively in police ears as it did in his own.

Peach certainly looked as if it did. 'These trials of adolescence. We see a lot of those. Sometimes we have to lock the little buggers up on account of them. Saving your presence, Vicar – sorry, Joe. Which ones did you guide Debbie Minton through? Drink? Drugs? Boys? Girls? Shoplift – '

'Debbie wasn't a bad girl!' Jackson interrupted the catalogue with a desperate insistence. 'We didn't see any evidence of drink or drugs here. I told you, not many of them come to the club once they're past about sixteen or seventeen.'

'So what were the particular troubles you held her hand through? Metaphorically speaking, of course.'

Now that the crisis was at hand, Joseph Jackson found himself strangely calm. It was almost like that dreaded first sermon which they had built up so much in the theological college. When the moment had come, he had been able to handle it better than the others. 'There was nothing too dramatic, Inspector. Debbie was a little too fond of the boys, but not unique in that.'

'And you were able to help her?'

Jackson took his time, as he had not been able to do earlier. 'I offered advice. Only she could tell you whether it helped her. She did come and talk to me on her own initiative, on several occasions.'

'And what was the subject of these little tête-à-têtes, Joe? You're not bound to secrecy, like the Romans, are you?'

Jackson smiled, feeling at last a degree of control. 'Even a Catholic priest is only bound to silence about the secrets of the confessional, Inspector. There is a lot of confusion about that. This was nothing like that. We had a few friendly talks, that's all. I felt she was being a little too free with herself.' He glanced at Lucy Blake; she thought afterwards that he almost seemed to know when he was going to produce one of her mother's phrases. 'There was a danger of her making herself cheap, I felt.'

Lucy said, 'How far did these liaisons go, Vicar? Was she sleeping around? Did you feel the need to speak to her parents?'

The clergyman seized almost eagerly upon the familiar question. 'I never speak to parents, unless it can't be avoided, in which case I warn the young person first of what I intend to do. So no, I didn't contact Debbie Minton's parents. I hope she wasn't actually hopping into bed with boys, but I can't be sure of it. If you put me on the spot, I'd have to say I believe she probably was, but I'm not certain of it.'

'With more than one? With several?'

Jackson was almost urbane in his regret. 'I fear so. That was the cause of my concern, you see. I don't know how successful I was in my efforts to divert her from this course.'

Peach said, 'Not very, from what we hear. Incidentally, she was pregnant when she died.'

Jackson raised his black-clad arms, steepled his fingers, pressed them together. He seemed about to offer some emollient platitude. Then he looked down at his hands and desisted hastily from what he saw as a cliché pose. 'I'm sorry to hear that. But don't forget this was two years after she had ceased attending our youth club.'

'So you've no idea who the father might have been?'

'No.' It came too quickly, without the pause for thought the question invited, so that what should have been merely a fact came almost like a denial. 'I've told you, I wasn't in close touch with Debbie by then.'

Peach let that hang for a moment, then said, 'We are questioning a lot of people, as you would expect in a murder inquiry. There seems to be some evidence that the girl also associated with older men. Could you give us a view of that, please?'

This time the colour rose rather than fell in the fresh, tell-tale cheeks. 'I don't have a view. When I knew her well, she only seemed concerned with her contemporaries. But girls develop a lot in the years from seventeen to nineteen, as you must be well aware. You'd do better to ask other people who knew her movements in those years.'

'Oh, we shall certainly do that, Joe. In fact, we've already started. It's surprising what we unearth, when we have the full resources of a murder inquiry to give to the job.'

Peach stood up, moving towards the door with his serg- eant at his side. As the vicar relaxed, he turned like a swift welterweight. 'We shall need a list of the people who were her contemporaries in your youth club. Girls as well as boys. Some girls of sixteen or seventeen confide everything to their girlfriends, as you in turn must be aware.'

The Reverend Jackson shut the door upon them before they had reached the last of the four steps. As Lucy Blake reversed the police car over the ecclesiastic gravel, they caught a glimpse of a white, oval face from a room above them which was probably the kitchen of the truncated vicarage. Mrs Jackson, presumably. She looked very much more anxious than curious. Lucy felt very sorry for her.

Peach felt a need to know how the woman beside him was reacting to his methods. They drove half a mile without a word. That was one of the things about women: they babbled away continually most of the time, but were quiet just when you wanted them to speak. Eventually he said, 'Do you think I was too hard on him?'

'Not for me to say, sir.'

'It is if I ask you.'

She turned a corner, braked briefly to avoid a kamikaze cat, considered her reply for fully thirty seconds more. 'Yes, if we go by the book, you were too hard on him. But it's not on tape, is it? And since you ask, I rather enjoyed it.'

'Why?'

'I should say because you seemed to be getting more out of him than by being polite. But really it was because I wanted to see him squirm. I thought he was a creep.'

Percy was delighted to find his prejudice echoed. 'Why?'

She gave a tiny shrug as she drove. 'The way he shook my hand. The way he took it in both of his, and held on a little too long. Female intuition, you might call it.'

He glanced sideways, studied her for a moment. He was able to do it more easily than ever before, because she was concentrating upon her driving as they approached a school crossing from which the lollipop lady had disappeared in the latest cuts. The nose on the firm, impassive profile turned a little upwards; the freckles at the temples were more noticeable from this angle; there was no smile upon the broad red lips. There was no tangible sign of amusement: he could not tell whether or not she was making fun of him. He looked back to the road ahead and said with satisfaction, 'We made the bugger jump about a bit, anyway.'

'We did indeed, sir!' Her relish seemed even greater than his.

CHAPTER ELEVEN

Christine Turner was a big success as Ladies' Captain of the North Lancashire Golf Club. Those men who were prepared to listen thought she had ideas which might well be of value to the future development of the club. Those diehards who considered women should be confined to the kitchen and the bedroom looked at her trim figure and her ready smile and thought her an appealing slip of a girl, even though she might well have been a grandmother by now.

But Christine was most successful with those who had chosen her to represent them, the ladies' section of the club. The old and infirm found her not only kind but mindful of past glories, when their limbs had been stronger and the world had been a kinder place. The good players found her both aware of their needs and able to compete with them; she was even on occasions able to emphasize that what they were about was after all a game, when they might have been tempted to take it too seriously.

The rabbits among the lady golfers (golf clubs have only ladies, never anything so dangerous as women) found her always ready with encouragement and understanding, and when necessary, with tactful guidance as to the arcane procedures in this most ritualistic of sports. She even contrived to encourage one or two teenage girls to take the plunge as golfing juniors into what would otherwise have seemed to them the forbidding blue-rinsed waters of the North Lancs.

But on this particular ladies' day, when her flock had the course to themselves for their competition, Christine Turner was preoccupied with other things. Only someone who knew her well would have recognized it. She made her usual brief but well-turned speech in presenting the prizes. She chatted with different groups as the decibel level rose to a shrill climax over the communal tea in the lounge. She made a point of going over to welcome back the lady who had just had the mastectomy and was sitting wanly cheerful over her tea and cake.

But Christine could not wait for this time she usually enjoyed to be over. She kept her eye on the clock over the bar, deliberately ignoring the neat gold watch on her wrist lest people should divine her impatience. As soon as she could do so, she slipped into the entrance hall of the club and made a call on the members' phone.

It took them some time to search him out, whilst she waited anxiously and smiled weakly at the few members who passed her. 'Francis? Thank God they've found you. Look, I must see you. You've seen the papers?' Even now, she felt she should not mention the name of Debbie Minton, as if that would somehow make things more damning for him. 'I need to see you . . . No, don't come here. I don't think you should be seen around here at the moment. I'll come and see you . . . No, not there. Somewhere more anonymous . . . Right . . . No, but I'll find it, if it's in the centre. Seven-thirty . . . ? And Francis, just don't say anything to anyone until I've spoken to you.'

She rang off and stared bleakly at the phone for a moment. Then she pulled her golf club cheer over her features and went back into the noisy lounge to make her farewells.

These two were a strange pair, thought Lucy Blake. She had almost got used to Percy Peach now, but his juxtaposition with Gary Jones still struck her as at once comic and a little sinister.

Perhaps that was because Jones was so patently frightened. When she had first entered the police force, she had been told that it was hard to be certain what a black man was feeling from his face. That was certainly not so in Jones's case. He was frightened, and it showed.

Not just ordinarily frightened; the young man seemed for the first few minutes to be on the verge of physical flight from them. Peach must have been conscious of his terror, but he did nothing to dispel it. Lucy knew the inspector well enough by this time to be fairly certain that he enjoyed it, that he was thinking of ways of fostering rather than diminishing it.

They had caught the young greenkeeper off his guard. He had been relaxing with his newspaper and the sandwiches he brought each day for his lunch in the big, hangar-like hut which provided shelter for both the course machinery and the course staff of the North Lancashire Golf Club. He was enjoying a few minutes' quiet away from the others; having worked later than his colleagues during the morning on clearing a particularly obstinate drainage ditch, he was dining alone after the others had gone noisily back to their work on the course.

Gary had worked hard with the trenching spade during the last two hours of the morning. He had enjoyed his sandwiches and the big mug of tea he had made himself as the others left. Normally he would have missed the gossip and the banter of his companions, but it was nice to have the place to yourself once in a while. He rocked contentedly backwards and forwards in the old chair. His eyelids began to droop as the warmth of the electric fire behind him stole over his tired limbs. There was a slight, not unpleasant smell of damp rising from the old carpet Tommy Clarkson had produced to cover the harsh concrete floor at this end of the big shed. In a moment, the newspaper slipped from between the slim fingers and drifted noiselessly on to the carpet.

'So this is where you're hiding yourself away. We thought you would have been back on the course with the others by now.'

Percy Peach's black leather shoes trod softly, and he had moved very close to the drowsing figure before he spoke. It meant that Jones, starting suddenly awake, saw the stocky figure framed in the light from the big open door as taller than it was, looming menacingly over him. It was so close that he had great difficulty in scrambling upright without touching this sinister new presence.

'I – I worked late this morning. I'm still on my lunch break, you see.' Gary peered at this menacing, bald-headed figure, who took care to stay between him and the light. Was it a member of the club? A new member of the Greens Committee perhaps, come to check on his staff? To report on the lad he mistakenly thought was a backslider? Most people were quite friendly when they passed him on the course, but Tommy Clarkson said there were still a few little Hitlers who got their kicks from a bit of authority. 'It's quite legitimate. If you ask Mr Clarkson – '

'I did, lad. And Mr Capstick in the clubhouse. That's why I'm here to have a word with you now. Assuming you're Gary Jones, that is.'

'Yes, that's me. But – '

'Police, lad. Inspector Peach. And this is Sergeant Blake.' Peach didn't trouble with a warrant card, not for a lad like this. For the first time, Gary became aware of the woman behind his awakener; she gave him a nod and a fleeting smile.

Peach moved closer still, so that Jones took an involuntary step backwards and stumbled over the leg of the old rocking chair he had been dozing in when they crept up on him. 'No need to be afraid, lad. Unless you've done something naughty, of course.' Peach managed to turn even reassurance into a threat. He looked at Jones speculatively from this closest of ranges, his bald head inclining a little to one side, like a healthy fox assessing the throat of a terrified chicken.

'Wh – what do you want with me?' Gary knew that he

should present himself better than this. He had been questioned by the police many times before; no black youth growing up in the town could have avoided that. He wanted to be truculent, as some of his companions had learned to be over the years. But he had never mastered that trick. And besides, these were plain clothes police, and that meant it was serious.

And Gary Jones knew already why they were here.

Peach looked unhurriedly round the shed, with its tractors and mowers, its chain saws, its fearsome-looking machine to spike the greens, its pile of fencing posts, its smells of grass and oil. 'Like working here, do you?'

'It's all right.' Gary tried the cautious surliness he had seen others use with the police. But his words seemed unfair to Tommy Clarkson and the others and he said, 'It's good here. We work hard, but it's in the open air and it's interesting work. And the boss – '

'You won't want to lose the job, then. No reason why you should, providing you give us your full co-operation. Unless, of course, you've been a seriously bad lad.'

Gary found that he had backed away to the bench against the wall: he could feel the steel handle of the vice pressing like a gun into his back. Peach must have followed him, for he was still very close, but Gary had never seen him move. He said, 'I'll give you all the help I can. But I'm sure – '

'Debbie Minton. That's what we're here about. To see what you can tell us about Debbie Minton.'

Gary swallowed, nodded. It was almost a relief that this menacing man had got to it at last. 'Is that the girl whose body we found when they blasted out the old quarry pond on the eighth?'

Peach smiled: a horrid, knowing smile. 'That's the one, lad. But what we're interested in is the people she knew when she was alive. The people she was close to in the months before her death. Including a certain Gary James

Jones. Very close to her, he seems to have been, at that time. According to our records at the station. According to other young men and women we have been talking to.' Best to feed that in now: saved a lot of time with denials.

Gary felt his knees trembling. He pressed back hard against the bench, finding the vice pushing his spine awkwardly forward. He must look as bent as some of the old men who played in the seniors' section on Wednesday mornings. Except that they usually seemed to be enjoying life, despite the restrictions of their infirmity.

He said, 'I knew Debbie, yes.' Then, with what seemed like a flash of inspired improvisation, he added, 'That's why I was so upset when we found what was left of her up there on the eighth.'

Peach's face broke into a slow, wide smile, the mirth spreading gradually over the squat features, until they reminded Gary of a long-forgotten illuminated turnip he had carried long ago on Hallowe'en. 'Mr Capstick and Mr Clarkson both noticed that. That you seemed unusually upset when those gruesome remains were discovered up there.'

The row of small, immaculately white teeth, with the two upper canines missing, seemed to be all that Gary could see at that moment. The rest of the face must now be perfectly visible in the light from the window at his back but that Cheshire-cat grin was all he could see. It deprived him of all power of thought, so that he blundered on, consolidating the mistake with which he had already delighted his tormentor. 'I was upset. I told you so. Finding Debbie up there like that really got to me.'

'Very understandable. Except, of course, that you shouldn't have known it was Debbie.'

'Shouldn't have known?' Gary heard himself stupidly repeating the phrase, like a television straight man.

Peach's grin disappeared as slowly as it had arrived; all humour seemed to drain with it, until the round white face of a tormenting ogre was restored. His voice was clipped, almost bored, as he said, 'We didn't know who it was ourselves for twenty-four hours. The identity wasn't released to the public until another day after that.' Without taking his eyes off his victim's face, Peach kicked the stool from beneath the bench out into the open. 'I should sit down, lad, if I were you. You look as if you need to. And we've hardly started yet.'

Gary sat down hastily, abruptly, deprived now of all rhythm in his movements. The stool jarred his buttocks, his hips, his whole frame, as if he had fallen on to it from a height. He gripped the edges of it as hard as he could, trying to feel the blood in the fingers, to give himself the proof that they were not actually as nerveless as they felt. 'I didn't know it was Debbie when we found her.'

'But you just said you did.'

'Yes. I – I was mistaken.'

Peach gave the tiniest of nods to Lucy Blake, which Jones did not notice because he had dropped his eyes hopelessly upon the cracks in the concrete floor. She said quietly, 'Then why were you more upset than the others, Gary? So upset that your boss and the club secretary noticed it.'

He looked at her in bewilderment; he had almost forgotten her presence during Peach's withering attack. 'I – I don't really know. I knew she'd disappeared suddenly and that no one had heard of her since then. I suppose I thought as soon as there was a body that it must be Debbie.'

He wondered how convincing it sounded. He was so disturbed by his own mistake and Peach's exploitation of it that he scarcely knew what he thought himself now, what was genuine and what he was fabricating in a desperate attempt to keep these people at bay.

Peach had withdrawn for a moment when his sergeant spoke. Now he returned with two battered chairs, which he set facing his nervous quarry. When he sat down beside Blake, his feet were so close to Jones's that the two sets of

toes almost touched. He said, 'Debbie Minton was murdered. You know that now. Maybe you knew a long time
ago.' He studied Jones, watching the young chin wagging
desperately from side to side. 'You won't be surprised to
hear that we're very interested in those who were close to
Debbie Minton in the months before she died. You were
one of them, weren't you? Perhaps the closest of all.'

'Not in that last month I wasn't!' His vehemence drove
out his fear for a moment, so that he was more definite than
he had been at any moment since they had surprised him.

Lucy Blake saw her chance to make him talk. 'Why was
that, Gary?' she said softly, easing forward on her chair,
using her proximity to encourage the slim figure rather than
to threaten him as Peach had.

Jones looked at her, at the freckled, unlined face and the
lock of dark red hair which escaped to flop towards her
deep green left eye. She was so close that he could smell her.
And she smelt nice: very fresh and clean. Gary wondered if
it was perfume, or just expensive soap. He warned himself
to be careful; he had never been questioned before by a
policewoman.

But he wanted to talk, despite this caution he urged upon
himself. 'She ditched me, didn't she? I hardly saw her during the last few weeks before she disappeared – not to speak
to, anyway.'

'Debbie was last seen on the twentieth of October, almost
exactly two years ago. She was killed very soon after that –
possibly even on the night she disappeared. How long before
that did you two split up?' She kept her voice even, unexcited,
concealing the fact that they had not even known just how
close was the relationship between this man and the dead girl
until he had unwittingly revealed it a moment ago.

'Five weeks.'

They noted the precision of that. He had not even needed
to think about it. 'Why did you split up, Gary? We need to
know.'

His fear had subsided now into a sullen exhaustion which had the resignation that Peach always liked to see: when people ceased to resist, information came quickly. He watched the boy's small, well-formed features as he strove to convince Blake of his integrity. 'We'd been very close, for a time. But I think now that it was really over before that. It was just quite a while before that final bust-up.' He suddenly sounded like a much older man; this earnestness issuing from the still very young black face would have been comic, if the issues had not been what they were.

It was Peach who said, 'You did drugs, Gary. We know that, because you were pulled in for questioning.' He had done his homework around the station before he came here. It never did any harm if suspects got the idea that the CID were omniscient. 'Did you introduce Debbie to LSD?'

'No!' This time Gary was conscious of how his denial rang round the huge shed like a shout of desperation. He tried hard to modulate his tone. 'I don't do drugs. I dabbled with them a bit, once. I didn't introduce Debbie to them. It was rather the reverse.'

'You're saying that when you were in trouble it was her fault?'

'No.' Why did this muscular, aggressive man have the power to turn everything he said to his disadvantage? It was like being cornered by a pit bull terrier. 'We all tried pot. Some went on to LSD or coke – '

'Like you.'

'All right. Like me. But when you warned me off, I listened.'

That didn't often happen, but perhaps it had this time. Certainly there was no evidence that Jones had incurred any further inquiries from the drugs squad. Lucy Blake said quietly, 'And did Debbie Minton listen, too?'

He looked troubled, as if even at this distance he did not want to betray her. But perhaps he was merely treading carefully, lest he accuse himself of a much greater crime.

'I think so. But she was into them before me. It was more curiosity than anything, for all of us. But drugs weren't important.' It was a familiar enough story. Young people experimenting with pot as with other things in life. Some desisting, some going on to other and more damaging things.

'You said you didn't split up over drugs.'

'It wasn't because I was black, either!'

Neither of them had suggested it was. But perhaps they had always had the unspoken question at the backs of their minds: at that moment, neither of them could have been certain whether or not that was the case. They waited with inscrutable faces, and Jones eventually said, 'It was other men.'

'Which other man in particular, Gary?' Lucy wondered if she sounded a little too eager; for the first time, she realized that Percy Peach, who trampled so mercilessly over his victims, knew also how to hold back.

'There wasn't any one in particular. Not that I'm aware of. She – she was just too free with her favours.' The old-fashioned phrase came so inappropriately from the frightened boy in that hangar-like setting that it should have been laughable. But he sat wretchedly with his head between his hands, and the four watching eyes were searching like lasers for a murderer; no one was inclined towards laughter.

Lucy waited for a moment before she said, 'Debbie was sleeping around?'

He nodded miserably, his head in his hands still, not trusting himself to speak. The tears were as near as if this had happened yesterday, not two years before. Peach was thinking of the first murderer he had arrested, who had cut his wife into pieces, dropped her in dustbin bags on to a waste disposal site, and then wept abjectly of his love for her as he had confessed.

Eventually Gary Jones said, 'I knew much earlier that it was over, really, but I suppose I didn't want to admit it.'

'You say there wasn't a particular man involved. But were there older men?' For a moment, Jones was silent, and she prompted him gently. 'We've already been told that there were, Gary.'

He looked up at her then. 'There were, yes. She taunted me that older men were so much less clumsy in bed than me.' The pain leapt on to his face at that remembered taunt, the worst a young man in love can have to endure. His observers shared at that moment the same thought, that such pain had often been the prelude to sudden, unpremeditated murder. 'Maybe there was one particular older man. But if there was, I don't know who it was.'

'Try, Gary. You want to know who killed her, just as we do. Do you think it was someone local? Someone with a position to keep up, perhaps?'

'She was secretive about him, whoever it was. She behaved as though there was something to be hidden.'

'And previously she hadn't troubled to spare you the details of her lovers?'

'No. I don't suppose she did.' He seemed to be seeing that distinction for the first time. 'But things moved quickly with Debbie. She was restless. "Trying to find myself" was the phrase she used to throw at me. I didn't even speak to her in the five weeks before she disappeared. She could have taken up with someone else entirely in that time.'

Gary was pleased when they had gone that he had given them that thought. It seemed to distance him, somehow, from this girl who had given him so much grief in life and now returned two years after her death to put him in danger. He sat alone for a long time in the shed before he could trust himself to move back into the bright daylight of the world outside.

In his room that night, Gary took the pewter brooch with its bright flashes of green glass from the back of the drawer and looked at it again. It seemed to have acquired an extra significance which came from outside itself, like the jewelled crosses and chalices he had once been taken to see in York Minster.

He could never forget now that this had been the brooch that Debbie had been wearing when she died.

CHAPTER TWELVE

Even policemen on murder investigations take some time off at weekends. They like to give the impression to the media that it is not so, that the hunt is relentless for twenty-four hours a day and for seven days of the week, but it is not really so. There are exceptions, such as those awful cases where children or young women are killed at random and everyone fears another killing is imminent. But Debbie Minton had died two years ago; there was little to be gained by going overboard on the overtime budget, however often Superintendent Tucker assured the public that no stone was being left unturned.

This meant that Detective Inspector Peach could become plain Percy and play in his first official competition at the North Lancashire Golf Club. He rang the young PC who had proposed him for membership and arranged to play with him on the Saturday afternoon. He would not normally have had the temerity to arrange to play with such a good player, but PC Bob Cook had seen the full range of his erratic golf on police society days at other courses. And he was Percy's proposer. And he was only a humble constable.

As the round proceeded, Percy began to wonder if he had after all made a wise choice of companion. Bob Cook was six feet tall, just under thirteen stones in weight, and twenty-eight. He was not only very fit, but very skilful. And he had played since he was five, so that Percy, despite being a decade and more his senior in years, was by comparison a fledgeling in experience.

Percy was quite satisfied with his opening tee shot – until Cook played. The younger man hit a long, low draw and finished some forty yards in front of Percy's suddenly puny effort. After Peach had hit a wood into the greenside bunker, his companion landed an effortless nine-iron within eight feet of the flag. The pattern for the day seemed to have been set.

Peach scrambled along and got a few putts in on the excellent greens. He managed nothing of great note, but he had no disasters. After seven holes, he found to his surprise that if he kept going like this, he would play very near to his modest handicap of sixteen. As a sport, this would never compare with cricket, but perhaps it wasn't such a bad way to spend Saturday afternoons in winter.

His companion's game was a thing of beauty, but Cook wasn't putting as well as he might, and he had a handicap of only three. When you took the handicaps into account, they were level pegging. That seemed ludicrous to Percy, who was used to games where the better player justly prevailed, but this was golf, so he gritted his perfect white teeth and concentrated.

It was as they played over the ruined quarry from the new tee on the eighth that Bob Cook played his first really bad shot, losing the rhythm of his swing and lurching into an ugly topped drive which barely cleared the new lake in the valley. Both their heads turned automatically as they trudged past the spot where the grisly remains had been discovered a week earlier.

'Did you know Debbie Minton?' said Peach.

'A little. I was working round here then, of course.' Bob Cook had been transferred some time earlier to a division some fifteen miles away, though he still lived in Brunton and played at the North Lancs.

Percy said, 'She was brought in for questioning once, I find. That must have been when you were here.'

'I think it was. She was questioned for being in possession of drugs. But there were no charges.' Cook strode off to the right, playing his second shot before Peach's second for the first time in the round. He seemed to Percy to play hurriedly, and thinned the ball again.

Percy, perhaps encouraged by this evidence of fallibility in his companion, managed to get his ball on to the edge of the green. Three minutes later, he managed to hole a four-foot putt to complete a very satisfying four. Cook then had his first three-putt of the day to finish the hole with an ugly six. He was very quiet for the rest of the round, whilst his score slowly deteriorated. Percy, recording the story on his card as they completed each hole, watched his companion pensively and speculated on the reasons for this decline.

When they had finished, Bob Cook looked at his watch as they went to their cars to put their clubs away. 'Took us longer than I expected,' he said. 'These medal rounds get slower and slower. I'm afraid I haven't time for a drink, Percy. Got the in-laws coming round for tea, so I'd better be away and get myself a few Brownie points. Would you put my card in for me, please?'

Peach looked thoughtfully after the car as the young man drove away. They had taken three hours to get round: Bob Cook could surely not have expected it to take much less. Policemen who could not dissemble better than that would never make the CID.

Percy handed in the two cards, finding almost as an afterthought that he had played one below his handicap. Probably he wouldn't win the medal, but it would be a respectable start to his golfing career at the North Lancs. He celebrated with a couple of drinks with two of the members he already knew, basking modestly in their congratulations, enjoying the humorous suggestions that his handicap was too high.

On his way home, he called in at the station. He knew which file he wanted, but without the help of the girls who were there during the week, it took him a little while to find it. He spread the sheet carefully on the top of the filing cabinet in the quiet room and studied it carefully.

The fact in itself was not so startling. It might be no more than coincidence. But Percy Peach had a healthy distrust of coincidence. He would certainly check this one out.

PC Bob Cook had applied for a transfer exactly three days after Debbie Minton had disappeared.

Percy Peach's Achilles' heel was middle-class, middle-aged ladies. He did not understand them. More importantly, he found it difficult to bully them, to give full rein to the belligerence which was a natural part of his interviewing technique.

Because of these things, they even scared him a little. He did not admit the fact, not even to himself, except when he lay awake in those small hours of the night which even the strongest and least sensitive of humankind have to contend with.

Christine Turner was not only an English middle-class lady but the Ladies' Captain of the North Lancashire Golf Club. Genghis Khan might have permitted himself a moment of uncertainty before that particular combination. In the various prisons of northern Britain, there were incarcerated a range of petty criminals who would have thought Genghis Khan was a pansy compared with Percy Peach. But they did not know about the middle-class ladies who were the Achilles' heel of their tormentor.

It was because he was secretly apprehensive about a confrontation that Percy broke his normal rules and sent Lucy Blake alone to see Christine Turner. 'I don't suppose there's anything there, but it has to be done. If you should turn up anything, we'll go back and see her together.' That was meant to keep his new detective sergeant in her place. She accepted the direction meekly enough, but she then went away with that secret smile which Percy was finding more disconcerting by the day.

If DS Blake held any inhibitions about middle-class ladies,

she was resolved that they would not show. But she went to see Mrs Turner at her place of work, and when she arrived there she was impressed, despite her determination not to be overawed.

Turner Home Services was a bustling and lively place. But it was predominantly a man's world. It sold tiles, cement, central heating equipment and most things that both the home handyman and the professional required for minor building works and extensions. Three men served and offered advice from behind a long counter which ran across the entire breadth of one end of the large single-storey building. Trade discounts were being calculated as Lucy slipped beyond this barrier and headed as she had been bidden to do for the door marked simply 'Mrs Turner'.

No 'Ms' in this man's world, she noticed. And certainly no phrases like 'Chief Executive' or 'Managing Director'. She half-expected to find the woman behind the door in a set of dusty overalls.

Instead, she found her in a green woollen dress that might have come from a fashion plate. Probably it was not really very expensive, but Christine Turner had the slender but not stick-like figure which might have been designed to model woollen dresses. Lucy decided enviously that even if she could afford the dress, she would never look as trim in it as Mrs Turner. She placed her own more sturdy backside carefully on the armchair indicated to her when she announced herself.

It was the kind of room that made you move with care. After the busy scene outside, it seemed almost unnaturally tidy. There was a fitted carpet, a desk, three armchairs, two filing cabinets. On the single windowsill, a busy lizzie flowered obstinately on into the autumn. Christine Turner disappeared briefly and returned with two china mugs of coffee on a small tray. 'Only instant,' she said with a grin, 'and no saucers. That's what the lads have, so it has to be good enough for us.'

Lucy grinned back and accepted the china beaker grate-fully. 'It's what I'm used to at the station. Except that here the crockery's better and the coffee's hotter.' She took one of the ginger nuts from the small, matching plate. Then she said, a little awkwardly, 'You run this place yourself?'

Christine grinned. This sturdy girl was half her age, but for a moment they were two conspirators in a world of aliens. 'My husband died four years ago. Everyone expected me to sell out. But I'd always been involved in the business and I knew most of the suppliers. Some of them thought they shouldn't be dealing with a woman but when they found I was getting prices from elsewhere they got the message.'

Lucy looked at the door to her right. 'It looks busy enough round your counter.' Then, fearful that this might be thought presumptuous, she added hastily, 'Not that I'd know anything about it.'

Christine Turner nodded, unable to keep the pride from her small, regular features. Then she forced herself to relax. Why shouldn't she show a little pride to this rare female observer? 'It's going well. It hasn't always been as easy as I have to pretend it is out there, but I get a lot of satisfaction out of it. Wherever Alan is now, he must have a laugh at me sometimes.'

Her face clouded for a moment, as the pain of her loss came unexpectedly back when she had thought it tamed. That often happened when she spoke about the business. Well, at least grief might take the edge off the nervousness she was so concerned to conceal.

As if in response to that thought, the eager-faced young woman who sat opposite her ended the preliminaries. 'I told you on the phone why I needed to speak to you, Mrs Turner.'

'Yes. Debbie Minton.'

'You knew her.'

'Yes. Quite well. I knew her parents, too. I saw her father at the golf club the other night. What the two of them must be going through! But I haven't seen her mother since the news came through.'

Because she was a woman not given to conversational ramblings, this came out as what it was, an evasion. And one which could not possibly succeed. Lucy Blake said, 'But you employed Debbie here, didn't you?'

'Yes. Not for very long, but we did.'

Why the disclaimer? She must know that they could easily find out for exactly how long. Lucy said, 'For almost six months, I believe.'

'Was it really as long as that? Time slips away when you get older, you'll find.' Christine Turner's giggle was brittle and entirely humourless.

'Why did she leave here, Mrs Turner?'

Christine thought for a moment of dissembling. She could say the girl found a better job, with more prospects. That she wanted female company. But it wouldn't be true, and these people would no doubt cross-check with others. Much better to keep as close to the truth as possible. So long as she could conceal the one connection that mattered. 'I had to get rid of her. It seems awful to speak ill of the poor kid now, but she – well, she was unreliable.' She knew that was a silly word as soon as she produced it. It merely invited further questions.

'She was a typist, wasn't she?' Lucy noted the tight-lipped nod from the woman who had been in such relaxed control when they spoke of the business. 'In what way did she prove unreliable?'

'There were a variety of ways. She became unpunctual, even after I'd warned her about it. You can't have a typist who takes liberties like that. In a small organization, other people soon begin to resent it.'

'We know that she dabbled with drugs. Perhaps more than dabbled – we still have several of her contemporaries to see about that. Did you see any evidence in her work of a serious drug problem?'

Christine managed a smile. 'You would be more expert about that than me. But now that you mention it, it could account for some of her more erratic behaviour.'

'There were more serious things than punctuality, then?' Lucy Blake's short, freckled face was studiously impassive, despite her obvious interest in the answers she was getting.

Christine Turner felt a sudden surge of resentment against this young woman who hid a penetrating mind behind the mien of a sixth-form hockey or netball player. But she must not get annoyed; mistakes came when you lost your calmness. 'There were, yes. Her work became a little sloppy. There were several occasions when I had to insist that she re-typed letters.' Then, because this sounded too trivial in her own ears, she added, 'And I'm afraid Debbie was becoming a disruptive influence.'

Lucy waited for her to go on. When she did not, she said, 'You must be aware that you can't leave it there, Mrs Turner. This is a murder investigation, and we need to know all we can about Debbie Minton. We already know quite a lot, so I doubt whether you are going to surprise me.'

Christine felt again that surge of hostility against this self-possessed young woman, who was calling the shots in this office where she was normally so much in control. But hostility would be not just illogical but dangerous. She strove to present the calmness she did not feel. She must make what she had to say sound convincing. 'Well, she was a little too keen on the men. One expects a little flirting in a place like this; even that a girl should enjoy being the centre of attention. But Debbie's conduct eventually began to affect not only her work but other people's as well.'

'She was making herself too freely available?' Lucy found that a useful phrase: she had picked it up from her first CID inspector.

Christine Turner nodded. She was finding this increasingly difficult, when as the older woman she should have been in easy control. It was in what she wanted to conceal rather than in what she was revealing that her difficulty came. She felt the tenseness in all of her body as she said, 'I heard one of the lads saying that she was "an easy screw". I've no doubt from what I saw of her at the time that he spoke the truth.'

DS Blake studied the taut, downcast face before her for a moment. 'We have had some evidence that the girl was consorting with older men as well as with people of her own age.'

Christine Turner looked up at her then, almost eagerly. 'Yes. I'd say from what little I saw and heard of her that that was almost certainly so.'

'Obviously we must follow up anyone who was in contact with Debbie Minton in the period before she disappeared and died. Do you know of any particular older man who was involved with her?'

The woman thought hard for a moment. 'No. I'm afraid I couldn't point to anyone in particular. I wasn't in touch with that side of her life, you see. I only saw her at work.'

'Nor any younger man who might have been close to her?'

'No. I – I didn't listen to gossip. I was only interested in her work and how that was affected.' Christine was not used to telling lies; her mouth set into an uncharacteristically hard line.

'Yes. I see.'

Lucy finished the exchange rather abruptly, wondering if more experienced interviewers would have managed things more smoothly. Not Percy Peach, she decided: he liked to leave people uncertain of their ground.

As soon as she was outside, she contacted the detective inspector on her car phone. He listened carefully to her account of the meeting. It was Lucy Blake's last words that interested him most. 'I deliberately didn't press her, because I knew we were going to see him anyway, and I didn't want to put him on his guard. She told me about how Debbie

Minton fancied anything in trousers. But she never mentioned her son.'

In his office in the CID section, Percy Peach put the phone down and stared at it thoughtfully. That was certainly an interesting omission in Christine Turner's account of things. There was almost something to be said for DS Blake, after all.

CHAPTER THIRTEEN

There was no question of making the phone call from home. Shirley did not go out on her own, even now, though she seemed better since the body had been found. Derek Minton, watching her with a fierce, hopeless love, thought he saw colour coming back into her face, and fancied that her shoulders were a little more erect. But how could he be sure? He was too close to her, too aware of her every thought, to be sure that it was not merely wishful thinking in him to see her moving back towards her old self.

He determined to make the phone call from work, but when the moment came he could not bring himself to do it, not even in the lunch hour, when the place was all but deserted. There was always the chance that someone would overhear him: he could not go through the switchboard, and he was never sure how secure these new-fangled phones were against eavesdroppers. Not at all, he fancied: you certainly felt exposed to the world around you when you stood with only the canopy of plastic above your head and shoulders.

So in the end he phoned on his way home from work.

The hour had gone back now, and it was dark when he slipped into the kiosk by the sub-post office. He pulled his collar up, like a seedy private detective, or a petty thief, or an adulterer. At any rate, someone who did not want to be spotted in this act; he knew that if he had been wearing a hat, he would have pulled it down automatically over his brow.

It was better than face to face, anyway. Perhaps the man he had to speak to would not realize how nervous he was, if he kept his voice steady. And indeed, as soon as he gave his name, he realized that the man who listened was more anxious than he was. The voice mumbled its sympathy over Debbie, but could scarcely get the words out. Conventional words, which a man like that must have mouthed on many occasions before. Yet he could not form them properly, and when he produced them they did not fall neatly into phrases as they should have done. The voice which faltered at the other end of the line might have been recovering from a stroke.

That frailty gave Derek Minton confidence. He issued his instructions with authority: his listener would never know how he had needed to nerve himself for this call. 'You and I need to meet.'

'I – I hardly think that will be helpful. I'm very sorry about Debbie, as I said, but – but I don't think it would be any use – '

'You saw her, just before she disappeared. Just before she died, it now seems. I know that, you see.'

'I – I don't see how you can – '

'She told me, you see. We talked a lot, my daughter and I. She told me where she was going, that last night.' Derek spoke with authority, with a massive confidence which was building on the other's uncertainty.

At the other end of the line, the man looked round the deserted hall like a hunted animal. He knew he was alone, yet the urge to check his surroundings, to make sure that he was not observed, was overwhelming. The very cupboards seemed to be listening, to be recording the agony of mind into which he had been plunged so abruptly. His voice rose towards a shout as he said, 'I can't help you, you know. And I swear I didn't – '

'No need to swear. We'll meet and talk about it. About what she said. About what you said. I'll come and see you there, if you like.' Derek knew that was cruel. He felt also his enjoyment in that cruelty.

'No!' This time it was a shout, echoing round the high cornice of the ceiling, returning like a blow to the ear which was not pressed to the phone.

'You can't come here. You must see that!'

'All right. You name the place, and I'll be there.'

For a moment, panic deprived his listener of all power of thought. He could think of no place and no time for this dreadful confrontation. His heavy, uneven breathing heaved down the line. Eventually he lurched into uneven phrasing. 'Half past eight. Tonight.'

'All right. The sooner the better. In a pub?'

'No!' He knew suddenly that it must not be inside, where others could observe his disintegration before the dead girl's father. He said desperately, blurting out the words as if he might at any moment be deprived of the power of speech, 'At the end of the shopping precinct. Near the entrance to the multi-storey car park.'

'Right. Make sure you turn up.' Derek Minton paused, savouring the final dagger of anguish before he thrust it home. 'I know all about you and Debbie, you see.'

Minutes after Derek Minton had left the public phone box and moved on towards his home, the man he had called stared unseeingly at the instrument which had brought this sudden horror upon him. He knew he must pull himself together quickly: his wife might return home at any moment. Yet the control his teeming mind desired would not come to him.

In the hall of the old vicarage, the Reverend Joseph Jackson dropped his face into his hands and wept.

Jeans everywhere. Pop music; the same programme from several unseen sources. Long hair, slim bodies, some but by no means all of them androgynous. A pervading stale smell of coffee and toast and beans. Percy Peach wrinkled his nose. 'What a lovely bloody life being a student. Bed, booze and pot.'

Lucy Blake said primly, 'The life has its own stresses. And there's not much pot nowadays. Not among British students. You'd soon smell it round here, if there was.'

Percy looked round the big room with its parquet floor, its cafeteria at one end, its strident murals on the other three walls. 'Bleedin' parasites,' he said without rancour; by now he was guying himself and the attitude he had adopted. 'I wouldn't mind a bit of this life myself. Don't know they're born, this lot.'

'You wouldn't be happy for one day, sir. Not without someone to order around.'

He glanced sideways at her. With the jeans and black leather jacket she had donned to come here, the dark red hair suddenly less disciplined than usual, she could have been a student herself. She looked younger in this gear; there was not a line on her face, her blue-green eyes were bright and observant. He felt a vague resentment that she should seem so much at home here. His own bald pate was probably the only one to have been in here all day: there was no sign of the mature students he was told were now such a feature of university life.

'Let's find the young bugger and get this over with,' he growled.

A young woman with blonde hair in a lengthy pony tail directed them without much curiosity to the hall of residence. They aroused more interest there in the acned youth who met them in the small entrance hall. 'Francis Turner? Sure, he lives here. What do you want with him?'

'Nothing that need concern you, sunshine. Just tell us where the lad resides and be on your way.' Percy bristled cheerfully at the sign of opposition.

The youth looked at him for a moment, then turned abruptly upon his heel and leapt up the stone stairs two at a time. Probably he thought he would leave them behind. If so he was disappointed. Peach accepted the challenge and almost overtook their guide: he was like a bouncing ball of muscle, thought Lucy Blake, as she flew behind him up the three flights.

It was the young Apollo rather than either of his followers who was panting when they arrived at a grey door with the number 317 upon it. He glared resentfully at the two bland faces beside him, then knocked at the door and threw it open. He stood in the entrance to the small room, so that they could not see what lay beyond him, and said to the invisible occupant, 'Visitors for you, Frank. Couple of pigs, I shouldn't wonder. Do you wish to see them?'

His four-square presence in the doorway did not survive this inquiry for more than a second. Peach slipped alongside the lanky figure. Then his shoulder caught the side of the thin chest, so that the acned guardian was bounced against the door-jamb and then somehow turned outwards. He stumbled against Lucy Blake, who returned him to equilibrium on the other side of the detectives, just in time to receive Peach's rejoinder. 'Lovely things, pigs. But dangerous animals when confronted in confined spaces. Might just be worth your while remembering that. Thanks for your help, sunshine.' He shut the door firmly on their discomforted guide.

In the small, square room there was a bed, a desk, two stand chairs, a single plastic-covered armchair. Hi-fi equipment, posters on the walls, books; even books that were open and in use. And in the midst of it, a youth, newly sprung to his feet. A young man with wide, fearful eyes.

'Do sit down,' said Percy, taking over as host in the man's own stronghold. As the student sank limply back on to the chair in front of the desk from which he had risen, Peach walked over and sat on the other chair, turning it so that his face was not more than three feet from his victim's as Lucy sank gracefully into the room's single armchair. Not a bad little room for this meeting, thought Percy, shifting his posture a fraction to allow the full light from the window behind him to fall on Turner's face. Not so very different from an interview room, when you organized it properly.

'First things first. You are Francis George Turner?' Nice touch of formality: students weren't used to that. Percy was a great believer in the power of the unfamiliar.

The slim young man nodded. Apprehension surged from his face through his whole frame, so that he could not find a comfortable position for his legs; they kept trying different crossings at the ankle, as if they moved independently of their owner.

'Then you'll already be aware why we're here.'

'Debbie Minton?' Francis tried to couch it as a question, but it emerged instead as an admission.

Peach said, 'Nasty business. Murdered. You'll be aware of that by now, if you weren't before.'

Before what, thought Francis. Then he realized what the implications of the remark were, and tried to stir himself to resistance. 'Listen, if you're suggesting that – '

'Suggesting nothing, lad. Not yet. We're here to find what you have to say for yourself. Then we might make a few suggestions.'

'Well, I knew the girl, yes.' The distancing suddenly made it sound cheap, as if he was dismissing her and everything there had ever been between them. That beautiful young face was suddenly before him, not dead but vividly alive, and he said, 'Knew Debbie, that is. Quite well, at one time.'

'Yes. We gathered that, from some of your friends in Brunton. Very close, weren't you, in the weeks before she disappeared?'

'Yes. Yes, I suppose we were. But I'm afraid I can't – '

'Strange that. Well, not that you should be close, but that someone should try to conceal it. DS Blake here saw your mother, you see. Only what we'd normally do, as she'd employed the deceased for six months. But your mother chose to tell us nothing of any liaison between you and Debbie Minton.'

'No. She wouldn't.'

'Really? Well, when people start concealing things, it's always of great interest to us, you see. They should realize that, but fortunately most of them don't.' Percy permitted himself a moment of satisfaction at the public's naivety.

'Mum didn't approve of me and Debbie.'

'And why was that?'

Francis Turner drew his over-active feet back under his chair and entwined them with the wooden legs, as if determined to immobilize them. 'She'd employed her. She thought she was too flighty.' It was his mother's word and it fell awkwardly from his lips.

Lucy Blake had confined herself so far to observing this young man under stress. Now she leaned forward on her armchair and said gently, 'She said as much to me, Francis. But she never mentioned that you'd even met the girl. That seems curious, when she obviously knew that the two of you had been quite close, and in the period which interests us.'

Francis seemed happy that she had come into the exchange. He was even anxious to explain himself to this apparently more sympathetic questioner. 'It was all right when we were just going around in a crowd. Mum got worried when we got a thing going with each other.'

Peach could not resist the opportunity. Indeed, he did not even try. He said, 'And she was even more worried when the two of you were pulled in for questioning about drugs, I expect.'

Turner whirled to confront him, his long face very white, his brown eyes blazing with resentment. 'There was nothing in that! And it wasn't just Debbie and me. Anyway, no charges were ever brought against any of us.'

'True. They could have been, though. You were in possession.' Peach looked briefly round the crowded little room. 'A promising academic career could have been blighted at the outset. You were lucky they were only interested in finding the suppliers, or you'd have had a record, lad.'

Lucy Blake said quietly, 'Is that what made your mother

so worried about your relationship with Debbie Minton?'

Francis found himself able to think when the questioning came from her. He even strove to be objective now about her query. 'It didn't help, obviously. But it was later that she got really worried.'

'You mean when you were having sex with her?' Lucy put it as simply as she could. And as accurately. Most people would have said 'sleeping with her', but from the parents' accounts of this girl's activities, she doubted whether this boy had ever had the luxury of actually sleeping with her.

He said, 'That's right. She warned me not to get seriously involved with Debbie. She was right, of course, but I wouldn't listen. You don't, at that age.' He spoke as if the time were two decades rather than two years behind him, as if he was looking back from middle age at the indiscretions of youth. Though he was not yet twenty-one, the two years that had concluded his adolescence stretched like a generation be-hind him.

Lucy said, 'You say your mother was right about Debbie, Francis. What made you see that?'

He paused, gathering his thoughts, organizing them into some sort of coherence. 'I'd been at public school. You don't learn much about girls there.' He permitted himself a wan smile at his own expense; perhaps he was recalling some far-off sexual indiscretion. 'Debbie was behaving like a tart, opening her legs to anyone who asked.'

Turner glanced at DS Blake, thinking in his naivety that she might be shocked, and found her instead impassively attentive. 'When I accused her, she admitted it freely enough. Said she'd enjoyed sampling my innocence. I'm sure that was a phrase she'd picked up from some book.' For a moment, his disgust at her plagiarism seemed greater than any sense of betrayal. Perhaps his contempt was really for himself, that he should have been so easily taken in by this shallow girl. They knew without him telling them that she had been his first sexual experience.

Lucy Blake, timing her line as carefully as any actor, said, 'Debbie Minton was pregnant when she died, Francis. Did you know that?'

'Yes.' Then, when they waited, he said, 'I read the report of the inquest.'

In the quiet room, they could hear the sounds of the pop music from a room a long way down the corridor. It was a raucous, incongruous love song. Lucy Blake said in what was little more than a whisper, 'But you knew much earlier than that, didn't you Francis? You knew before the night when Debbie Minton disappeared.'

There was a pause which stretched into several seconds, until they thought he might say nothing. Then he said, in a voice as low as hers, 'Yes. I knew.'

'And were you the father of that child, Francis?' She was like the priest in the confessional, quietly leading the penitent on, until the full depth of his sinning should be quietly revealed. Except that there was no privacy for the secrets of this confessional.

'I could have been. I don't think I was, but I could have been.'

There was a kind of relief that it was out at last: that too was like the confessional. Beyond the double-glazed window, two men were teasing a pretty female student; it was the silent horseplay of a different world.

It was almost as an afterthought that Francis Turner looked from Blake back to Peach and said, 'I didn't kill her, though.'

CHAPTER FOURTEEN

Lucy Blake was quietly pleased with herself. Peach seemed to approve of the way she had handled Christine Turner earlier in the day. And now he had let her play a major part in the questioning of the woman's son. She checked her reactions. It wasn't the male approval that pleased her; it was the professional approval. Peach was her boss, infinitely more experienced in the techniques of detection than she was. So that was all right, wasn't it?

As they marched briskly to retrieve Peach's Sierra from the university car park, she was almost stopped in her tracks. For Percy Peach, male chauvinist and expert in arrogance, said suddenly, 'Fancy a drink, Sergeant?'

She managed to disguise the slight check in her step, so that she was alongside him again almost immediately. She glanced surreptitiously at the stubby profile. There was no sign of irony there; Peach was gazing resolutely ahead, as if the tower of the administrative block was suddenly of consuming interest to him. Had she not known him to be proof against anything so human, she might have thought he was embarrassed.

She said, 'I'd love to, sir. On two conditions.' Could it really be her who had said that? She was astonished at her own temerity.

Peach seemed not at all surprised. He kept his gaze glassily on that high brick tower to his left. 'Well?' he grunted.

'First that you call me Lucy, at least in the pub. Second that you let me buy.'

For a moment, she thought he was going to erupt. Then he said gruffly, 'Fair enough.' After another few paces, he said, 'Never known to refuse an offer like that, Percy Peach. And you must call me Percy, of course. Everyone else does.'

But not necessarily to your face, thought Lucy, thinking of the awe and fear which attended the mention of his name in the locker rooms of the Brunton cop-shop. There seemed nothing else to say after this momentous exchange and they walked on without words, neither of them daring to look at the other's face. She was glad when they reached the pub. They wheeled into the public bar in parallel, like thirsty soldiers after a long march.

Lucy went to the bar, wondering now why she had insisted on buying. He must be laughing up his sleeve at her — if you could really do that. Perhaps she was getting more butch by the day, as she strove to hold her own in this predominantly male environment. She'd be flexing her knees and loosening her underpants next. Just so long as Detective Inspector Percy Peach didn't try to loosen them for her.

Good job he couldn't read these insubordinate thoughts. She looked back towards where he had seated himself carefully in an alcove. In his neat suit and tie, with his immaculately groomed hands and his jet-black fringe of hair beneath the shining pate, he could be industrial middle-management relaxing after a day at the office. Seeing what he could get from a bird from the typing pool, perhaps.

Except that she was no typist. And Percy Peach was surely not interested in anything he could get from her. And he was not so much older than her, anyway. Ten years was not much of a gap, all the magazines said. It just seemed a gulf because he had been at this work so much longer than she had.

She took him his pint of bitter and set her own half down precisely opposite it, as if to emphasize her femininity. Then she realized that beer, even in halves, was hardly going to do this. Perhaps it might make her one of the boys. She would welcome that, surely? Hadn't she spent most of her time in the police force striving for just that acceptance?

Peach took a pull at his bitter, then afforded it a small grimace, which seemed to mark a guarded approval. 'Well, did he do it?' he said abruptly.

'Francis Turner?'

'Who else, Sergeant? Lucy.' He produced her name like a man getting rid of a mouthful of something he found overwhelmingly sweet.

She thought about it for a moment, resolutely thrusting away her amusement at his difficulty with her name. 'Possible. He didn't come forward when he knew we were looking for people who'd been close to her. Both he and his mum failed to behave as responsible citizens should – more like ordinary people, they were.' She looked at him for any sign of amusement, but his round, intent face did not smile. 'If he was the father of Debbie's child – and I'm not sure he was as uncertain about the parentage as he protested himself to be – I'd say he's definitely in the frame.'

'Too many ifs,' said Peach, as if that were her fault. 'What about the mother?'

'Christine Turner? I scarcely thought of her. She seems – well, somehow too much in control of her life to attempt murder.'

'Whoever killed Debbie Minton was pretty much in control. Without the accident of someone decided to demolish that old quarry pool, they'd almost certainly have got away with it.'

Lucy said slowly, 'A mother in defence of her child might do all sorts of things she wouldn't do for herself.' She was thinking of her own quiet, conventional mother, of the way she had stormed into her school with astonishing aggression when her eight-year-old daughter was being bullied. And Francis Turner was the only son of a widowed mother.

'And she needn't have killed the girl herself you know,' said Peach with satisfaction. 'Women like her always have resources available to them,' he added mysteriously.

Lucy didn't want it to be Christine Turner. And because she had liked her, she didn't want it to be her son. It was a wholly unprofessional attitude to bring to her first murder inquiry. Fearful lest Peach should divine her thoughts, she said a little desperately, 'What about Derek Minton?'

Peach looked up from his beer with a little smile of surprise, and she was fearful that he had read her thoughts about the Turners. But he seemed to approve of her suggestion, for he said, 'Always a good principle to start with the next of kin. Statistically, at any rate, they're the best prospects.'

'But I couldn't see either of the Mintons being involved. Shirley's suffering has been too long and too well documented to be anything but genuine, surely?'

'Agreed.'

'And I'd say they were too close-knit a family for it to have been Derek. He's suffered with his wife – watching her pain, I mean. I think he's too much in love with her to have done anything to her daughter, Percy.' She tacked the appendage on to the end of her sentence, hoping it did not sound as clumsy to him as it did to her. At least it might stop him questioning her about how she had divined that a husband was in love with his wife.

He said only, 'You're probably right. The only thing I would say is that it's in those families where emotions are most intense that you get violence. So the statistics about manslaughter and homicide tell us. So we should keep Minton in the frame, for the moment.'

Without asking her, he went to the bar and ordered the same again. It was what he would have done with a man, she supposed. She was still not sure whether she found that thought a consolation or not. 'Bet they think in here that I've picked a student up!' he said when he came back and set the drinks on the table. For the first time, he looked openly at her jeans and leather jacket, her shirt with all its buttons save the top one modestly buttoned. 'Your clothes are a bit too clean for that, though. And I need to grow a beard before I could be a tutor on the make.' He grinned his beaver's grin and put his ankle on his knee for a moment, as if experimenting with what he considered an academic pose.

Lucy did not know what to make of this. She said, diffidently, 'There's Gary Jones, of course.' Then, because Peach said nothing, seemingly occupied with the depth of the foam on the top of his pint, she added, 'The coloured lad on the ground staff at the North Lancs.'

'Greens staff they like to call it. Same difference.' He took a pull at his pint, as if finally accepting that he had not received short measure. 'Statistics again: much higher incidence of violent crime among blacks than other immigrant groups or native whites.' He used a soppy, high-pitched voice for this, and she knew that he was teasing her.

Nevertheless, she rose helplessly to the bait. 'Among the deprived, you mean. Urban black people have bad accommodation and wretched employment prospects, even when they've lived all their lives here. It's no wonder they loom large in the serious crime statistics.'

'Quite right, quite right.' He grinned at her, enjoying her earnestness, not putting her down. 'But when you confront a crowd, it's easier to see a black face than deprivation, so one takes note. Lucy.'

'Gary Jones was certainly frightened. Probably not just of us. Percy.' She found herself enjoying this mixture of business and sparring.

'No. He was scared as soon as they found the body. Perhaps even before they found it, if what his boss says is true. If it is, that might indicate that he knew the body was in the quarry pond.' This time he did not append her name in that tantalizing way. This time he was deadly serious.

She thought of that delicately handsome face, of Jones's slim figure, of his eagerness to please. They all said at the golf club that he was a model employee. That he might go far in greenkeeping, with his enthusiasm and intelligence. That he might break out of the deprivation she had been pleading for his colour. Unless, of course, he was a murderer.

She said, 'He had a close relationship with Debbie.'

Peach grinned at her formality. 'He was knocking her off, yes, for a period. So were several others. He seems to have been a bit more serious about her than most. Perhaps he took it badly when she nipped into the sack with others.' He looked at her across the top of the glasses, stubby chin jutting as if in challenge to her sex. 'This case might have been straightforward, if Debbie Minton hadn't been such a slag.'

She wondered why there was no term for a man who put himself about like that. Because the men devised the terms, she supposed. But she forced herself to look at the matter as a good detective sergeant should. 'There might not be a murder investigation at all, without that. But Debbie's a victim, whatever her sexual habits, Percy.'

This time the name came almost naturally. He said, 'Of course she is. And without victims, we wouldn't have a job. Gary Jones is our strongest candidate, at present. His friends say that he was far gone on the girl. Quite starry-eyed about her. He still seems a bit young for his age to me, and this was over two years ago. I can see him doing stupid things then.'

Lucy Blake looked miserably at her still untouched second glass of beer. She still didn't want it to be Gary Jones. She supposed that she would become more objective with experience. Assuming, that is, that she was allowed to gather it. Trying hard to sound enthusiastic about the recollection, she said, 'Jones did tell us about how she taunted him about his performance in bed. That bites deep with men – I imagine.'

He looked at her when she made this hasty addendum, and found her blushing to the roots of her dark red hair, her freckles only highlighting the pink around them. She was furious with herself as she felt the blood rise, but she had always had to contend with the phenomenon; it was something that went with her colouring, they said. Fat lot of consolation that was. She half expected Peach to make fun of her, and knew she would explode with fury if he did.

Instead, he said, 'He wasn't the only one to mention an older man. Wonder who it might be? Or whether, knowing our Miss Minton as we are beginning to do, there was more than one older man?'

'It could be someone we don't even know about. Someone no one has mentioned yet, from outside the area.'

'Of course it could. But if she was killed on the night she disappeared, which seems more and more likely, that is much less probable.' Peach paused, then sipped his beer. It appeared no more than an appreciative moment, but he was coming to a decision; one he would not have made a week earlier. 'There are two candidates I can think of for the old man role. Even leaving out Derek Minton. The first one you don't even know about.'

She looked her question, feeling the fire subsiding in her cheeks, grateful that he had chosen not to comment upon it. 'But I'm about to learn?'

He grinned, a little boy's grin, his small white teeth briefly fully visible. 'Would I ever keep things from my DS? But not a word to anyone about this. Least of all to Tommy Tucker. You'll see why in a moment. It's a policeman, you see, Lucy.'

She was so surprised that she scarcely noticed how naturally her name had come this time. 'Is it someone I know? Someone at Brunton?'

'No. Someone who used to be. Chap called Bob Cook. PC Bob Cook. Aged twenty-eight. Married, with two kids. Good golfer, very good. Proposed me for the North Lancs.'

He took a ruminative pull at his pint, as if meditating upon the ironies of life.

'And is his golf relevant to this case?' She was ribbing him a little, mocking the preoccupation with the game she chose to detect in him. But in fact, he did not speak about it at all at work. And he certainly did not sneak off to play when he should be working, like Superintendent Tommy Tucker, who kept a putter in the cupboard in his office to practise on the carpet when he thought he was protected by the light outside his office which announced he was Engaged.

Percy took her question seriously. 'It might be relevant that Bob Cook knows the North Lancs course so well. He's played there since he was a boy. So he would know all about the existence of that old quarry and its pond. Whoever dumped Debbie Minton's body in there didn't come across that pond by accident on the night: it's far too remote.'

'But there has to be more against him than that. Otherwise the whole membership would be suspect. Including one Percy Peach.'

She could not resist looking at him to see how he took that. He was looking hard at her, as if he had been waiting for her scrutiny and found it amusing. His dark, almost black pupils were wider than usual in the subdued light of the pub alcove. There was a glint of mirth in them, and he smiled, appreciatively, not wolfishly, as he did when in pursuit of victims.

Then his face became serious. 'I hope to God it isn't Bob. But he did know the Minton girl. And he didn't want to talk about her. And last Saturday, his golf fell apart when we got to the point on the course where her body was found. So I checked his record at the station. Did it myself, it being a Saturday afternoon, without even the assistance of my trusty DS.' He checked automatically that they were not overheard, then leaned forward and said to her, 'No one else knows this as yet, Lucy. But Bob Cook applied for a transfer three days after the night when Debbie Minton disappeared.'

She stared glumly at her half-empty glass. No one likes a bent copper, and she had absorbed enough of the tribal ethos to be as disturbed as the most grizzled station sergeant by the idea that one of their own might be a murderer. She said, 'What do we do next? Question him further?'

'Yes. But discreetly. If it becomes clear he's guilty, we throw the book at him, of course. But if he isn't, we must be careful not to affect his future career in the force.' He wondered if she thought it was men looking after men, prepared to cover over sexual transgressions if they proved to be no more than that. A week earlier, probably two days earlier, he would not even have considered her reactions, let alone cared about them.

She was thinking of the wife and two young children, of the shattering of this family she did not even know if Bob Cook should be involved in this. It would have surprised her to know that Peach was thinking about them, too. They were the chief reason for his warning that they must proceed with discretion. A copper who had behaved stupidly, even if not criminally, would get the normal robust treatment he meted out to the venal and the foolish, but there was no reason for his innocent dependants to suffer.

Peach said, 'I'll set up some kind of meeting with Bob Cook. Preferably not on police premises. I . . . er, I'd like you to be there.'

This time the dark eyes were staring resolutely at the period mirror on the wall advertising Wills' Woodbines. She had the sense to say no more than, 'Of course.' She feared she would blush again, and was glad when he pressed quickly on.

Perhaps he too was anxious to dismiss the moment, for he said with abrupt satisfaction, 'What about the Reverend Joseph Bloody Jackson?'

'You think he might be involved?' She asked it stupidly, with her mind still on the previous exchange. It was an amateur's reaction, and she hastened to cover it. 'I mean, he was certainly a bit creepy, but I doubt whether he had it in him to be a murderer.'

It sounded banal in her own ears. But this was her first murder investigation, so that she could perhaps be forgiven for producing the layperson's stock reaction to killers.

Percy Peach merely smiled, where once he would have snarled. He found this mildness a little disturbing in himself but he pressed on with his demolition of the clergyman. 'He's a bit free with his attentions to the girls in that youth club, according to what the team have turned up in their questioning of Debbie Minton's contemporaries. And Debbie seems to have been pretty free with herself. If Jackson had his hand up her skirt, God knows what could have happened afterwards. And unfortunately God doesn't grass on his workers, even when they let him down.'

He wondered if she might object to the way he spoke of Debbie Minton, if she might point to her youth and the weight of guilt upon any older man who traded upon her weaknesses. Instead, she said, 'I can see how Debbie might have rather enjoyed a situation which would have frightened other girls. And we do have the mention from several sources of this mysterious, so far unidentified older man in the background.'

'There are two things about that. First, if he exists, and he probably does, there is no necessary reason why he should be Debbie's killer. Rather the reverse: youngsters like Gary Jones and Francis Turner are more likely to be panicked into sudden, violent action than an older man who might have been after a little cheap fun. And secondly, we have to remember that the mention of an older man comes from Debbie herself, who was no more than nineteen at the time of the relationship. Bob Cook, who seems to me quite young, has a wife and children. He might well be seen by a girl of Debbie's age as an older man.'

'So Joseph Jackson isn't the only candidate for the role. Just the one you'd like it to be.' She grinned across the table, daring him to challenge this slur on his objectivity.

He grinned back, then intoned in a pious, pulpit voice, 'If Joseph Aloysius Jackson is soiling the honest young women of this parish, it is our bounden duty to protect our young English roses.'

'Even if they guided the ecclesiastical hand up their provocative skirts and into the confines of their too scanty drawers?'

'Our English roses would never do that. We shall need to have further discussions with the Reverend Joseph Jackson.' Peach's expression left no doubt that it would be a pleasure as well as a duty.

They did not speak much as they drove the thirty miles back to Brunton. He dropped her off at her flat. He leaned across from the driver's seat to look at her front door as she got out, but neither of them made any suggestion that he should come in. Perhaps both of them were a little relieved that the day was at an end.

CHAPTER FIFTEEN

At the very moment when Peach and Blake were deciding that the Reverend Joseph Jackson merited their further
attention, Derek Minton was preparing for the meeting he
had compelled upon that unhappy clergyman.

He did not leave his wife often in the evenings, and since
Debbie had disappeared Shirley had ceased to work at the
supermarket which had kept her out on three evenings of
the week. It was no hardship for him to stay in with the wife
he loved, particularly now that she was showing signs of
returning to normal. He was not a drinking man, nor one
who sought the company of his own sex as a respite from
domesticity.

He had always been keen on sport, but he had given up
his tennis and badminton after Debbie disappeared, pleading that he had always meant to desist when he reached
fifty, and that forty-six was near enough to that, in these
circumstances. The truth was that he had not wanted to
leave Shirley, feeling that she was alone enough during the
day in any case; that his presence, even in those dark
months when she had stared unseeingly at the wall, was
some sort of assistance to her.

But he had kept up his membership of the North Lancs
Golf Club, playing a little even when things were at their
worst, when every leaf in the garden had been in place and
that tidy house had become like a prison, with the wife he
loved as its silent sentinel. He was not a bad golfer, and he
was surprised how much he enjoyed those rounds he stole
as therapy. And after he had played, he kept his ears open as

he sat over his modest half of bitter in the bar, feeling obscurely that there might eventually be news of Debbie here.

And in the end, there had been news. Perhaps, indeed, the golf club, being the place where she had been found, was still the place to gather news: wasn't that sinister little bull terrier of a man who was pursuing the investigation now a member of the North Lancs?

It was that thought which gave him his excuse to leave the house. 'I think I'll just pop up to the golf club for half an hour,' he said to Shirley. 'See if I can fix myself up with a game at the weekend – the starting-time sheets might be up for the November medal.'

She looked at him curiously, a little smile twisting her pale lips. He had always had the feeling that she could see through his lies, but perhaps that was merely his imagination. It was good to see her alert and showing some interest in his movements, at any rate. It was curious how the awful news about Debbie's body had initiated a slow revival in her. Perhaps she was glad to see him going out to the place where Debbie had been found. Perhaps, in a few months, they would be able to get back to a normal life together. Once the search for their daughter's killer had been brought to a satisfactory conclusion, that is.

Wasn't that what he was about tonight? And didn't that justify his small white lie to the woman he loved? Sometimes events had to be given a little push forward, that was all.

Derek took care to turn towards the golf club when he backed the car out of the garage, just in case Shirley should be watching him from the house. But when he reached the end of the road, he turned the Astra in the other direction, towards the town centre. He looked at the clock on the dashboard as the tall shadow of the multi-storey car park loomed through the urban darkness. It was eight thirty-seven. He was seven minutes late; that was exactly what he had planned. Let the slimy bugger fret for a little while in the shadows. This business was going to turn out all right, after all.

He had no trouble in parking on this midweek evening. The air was still with an autumnal cold: there would be a frost before morning. Even the weather was supporting his purposes; there were few pedestrians about to observe this meeting, and those who were abroad hurried about their business with their collars raised against the cold.

As he passed the lighted windows at the end of the pedestrian precinct and moved towards the appointed spot, a chill gust swirled between the tall buildings, ruffling the inevitable crisp bags and cigarette packets even on this still evening. He did not see Jackson at first but that did not worry him. He knew the man would keep himself invisible for as long as possible, but he was confident his quarry would not dare to deny his summons to this meeting.

He was right. The Reverend Joseph Jackson came suddenly forward from a shop doorway, his right hand clutching his coat tight against his throat. Derek knew in that instant that he was wearing his dog collar, that he wished to conceal this mark of identity from any curious observer. Perhaps, thought Derek, he wished at this time to deny it even to himself. The thought gave him even more confidence: Minton's colleagues in the council offices would have been surprised to see the confidence, even truculence, in this man who was so retiring by day.

The clergyman said, 'You're late.'

'Only a little. Sorry if you've felt the cold.'

As if the words had cued it, Jackson was shaken by an involuntary shiver. 'I don't see the need for this cloak and dagger stuff.'

Derek smiled, turning his head a little so that his face got the full light from the high lamp above them, making sure that Jackson could see the smile with which he accompanied his shrug. 'You wanted us to meet here, not me. I was happy to see you at the vicarage, or in a pub.'

Jackson's miserable nod of assent turned into a shudder, as he contemplated again the horror of a meeting in either of those places. He thrust his hands deep into the pockets of his dark overcoat and said unwillingly, 'What is it you want with me, anyway?'

'I think you know that. I want to talk about our Debbie. About her relationship with you. And about why she wanted to see you on the night she disappeared.'

Jackson tried hard for a return to the avuncular manner he adopted for his parish visits. 'I – I don't know where you've got the idea that I can help you, Mr Minton. I told you, I'm very sorry about Debbie, but – '

'But you'd like to forget all about her. To pretend you hardly knew her. Perhaps to bury what's left of her, in due course. And then to breathe a sigh of relief, and quietly forget about her!'

The vicar started, glanced over his shoulder, clutched again at the clothing about his neck. It was so near to what he had been thinking since the discovery of the girl's remains that he could summon no breath to deny it. Derek noticed how pale his large face was as it caught the light. Normally it was rubicund, as if his professional cheerfulness and benevolence had sunk beneath the skin to produce the appropriate colouring.

Joseph Jackson had to lick his lips before he could say, 'I think you've got the wrong idea from somewhere about Debbie and me. She – she was just a member of the church youth club, like many other young people of her age. I hope she enjoyed herself there, of course.' He had prepared this before he came. Because Minton did not interrupt him, he gathered a little strength and pressed on with the phrases he had considered so carefully. 'She was a lively girl, and we all enjoyed her company. But in due course, as is the way with these things, she moved on to other – '

'Some people enjoyed her company a little too much. Including some who should have known better. Including the vicar in charge of the club. A man of the cloth, who should have known better.'

'But I can assure you that – '

'You can assure me of nothing. Because I know, you see. Know all about you and our Debbie.'

'Debbie was an attractive girl.' Jackson found Minton had begun to move away from him, down the side street which ran by the side of the multi-storey car park, into the large pool of shadow where one of the lights was not working. Jackson followed him, because he could do nothing else.

He felt certain that this intense, threatening man would turn to physical violence if he chose the wrong words now. The thought distracted him, making what he was trying to say even less effective. 'I'm sorry to have to say this, Derek, but she was – well, a little promiscuous.' He stopped, studying the shoulders in front of him for some sort of reaction, wondering when he least wanted to whether it was even possible to be 'a little' promiscuous. He tried to appeal to reason, but his pleading rose almost to a whine, 'Debbie had plenty of young boys of her own age interested in her. Why should she be interested in an old fogey like me?'

Minton whirled upon him then, catching Jackson with arms outstretched in entreaty, so that the dog collar he had been so anxious to conceal was for the first time revealed, even in that gloomy place; a brighter band of white against the pale flesh of the throat behind it. 'Only she knows that. And she isn't here to tell us, is she? Minister?'

His voice turned into a snarl on the last word, so that Jackson was consumed not just with the fear of discovery but of being struck by the man confronting him. He scratched desperately at his panicking brain for the phrases he had prepared in his study during the afternoon. 'You're not in a position to be objective about your stepdaughter's conduct, Derek. That's understandable, but – '

'I know all about you and her, Jackson. You had your

hand up her skirt when she was no more than a kid. She told me, you see. Not at the time, but afterwards, when she saw you for what you were. When she was able to be "objective" about randy men in cassocks.' He flung Jackson's own word back into the pale oval of his face like a blow, feeling the surge of excitement when it flinched from him in the darkened street.

Jackson felt his head swim. He felt now that he had known from the start that he could only be defeated in this contest. Yet the stakes were too high for him to lose. He knew suddenly that if this was not over quickly, he would collapse, here on the street, in the centre of the town. If only the girl had not been at once so desirable and so available; he had never met that combination before. He said hopelessly, 'What do you want from me?'

Derek Minton knew that he had his victory now. He must keep his head, though, if he was to extract what he needed from it. 'I want to know what happened at the end. That last night, when she came to see you.'

Jackson had not expected this. He found his racing mind could not cope with the unexpected. He had thought the angry father would press him for the full details of what he had done with the girl. Indecent assault, they called it, didn't they? Or was it worse than that? Would it be in his favour that there had been no actual penetration? Or were all these things called sexual acts, nowadays?

His first reaction to Minton's question was one of relief that it was about that last brief meeting, that he was not to be pursued on the physical details of what he had done with that wretched, forthcoming, smiling girl in those earlier months. Perhaps, if he could provide this avenging angel with the answers he wanted, he might after all escape without physical assault. 'I – I can't remember, exactly. It's two years ago.'

'Try. Now.' The monosyllables came at him like bullets.

'Well, I hadn't seen her for quite a long time. Then she

saw me in the street and stopped to talk. That would be about a week before – before she disappeared.' He was expecting to be interrupted, to be badgered, to be contradicted. He found the concentrated silence of his interrogator almost more unnerving than his aggression had been. He could see only the outline of the wiry Minton in this darkened street. The man was like a panther, waiting to pounce on a wrong move by his victim, thought Jackson. 'She was different. Quieter than I remembered her. She was quite a bit older, of course. She said she'd like to come and talk to me some time.'

'And she did.' It was quiet, a prompting rather than a threat.

'Yes. She came, as you said, on the night when she disappeared.'

'And she told you things.'

'No.' His denial came too quickly. He felt absurdly like Peter denying his Christ. If Christ was everywhere, as his ministry preached, then perhaps it was the Christ in that wretched girl that was calling out to him. 'At least, nothing that can help you much in the search for her killer.'

There came a sound through the darkness from the other man. It might have been a sigh of resignation. It might as easily have been a gasp of disbelief or outrage, and Joseph Jackson hastened on to justify himself, 'She said she was desperate, or she'd never have come to me.' That much, at least, must ring true, he thought abjectly. 'She said there was an older man. She wanted to get rid of him, but she didn't know how to go about it.'

'What was his name?' The small, fierce face of Derek Minton came out of the shadows to within a foot of the vicar's larger one. Jackson could even see the glittering blue of the eyes; they were on a level two inches below his own, and they seemed to have drawn into themselves all the scanty light of that shadowy place.

'She didn't tell me that.'

Those glittering, scarcely human orbs tunnelled into his face for a minute, then apparently accepted it. 'What about her pregnancy?'

'She – she didn't tell me about that. I – I sort of half guessed, I suppose, from other things she said.'

'Who was the father?' There was a pleading note suddenly about the sharp features so close to his, but Jackson had no information to give. 'I don't know. Really I don't. She didn't even acknowledge openly that she was pregnant.'

'Was it this older man?'

'I – I don't know. It could have been. Or the child could have been a younger man's. Perhaps that's why she wanted the older man out of the way. But I couldn't say. At the time, I didn't know I wouldn't see her again.'

'What advice did you give her?'

Jackson felt almost easy about this; what he had to say must surely be acceptable. 'I said she should discuss her problems with her parents. She laughed and said that wasn't on. That's why she'd come to me, she said. I'm afraid a lot of girls won't reveal their troubles to their parents, even when we think they should.' For a moment, he might have been consoling a distressed mother over the teacups at the vicarage.

'Did you kill her?'

The words were so quiet, so matter-of-fact, that Minton might have been inquiring about the time of a weekend service. Something warned Jackson that the speaker was exercising supreme control, which might break at any moment if he made a wrong move. 'No. I swear I didn't.' He could feel the sweat upon his forehead, even on that bitter evening. It cooled even as it arrived, as if someone was sliming his brow with crystals of ice.

'You'd better be right. You seem to have been the last person to see her alive. The police would certainly be interested in that. But perhaps you shouldn't tell them about that. Unless your conscience tells you to do it, of course.'

The contempt came at Jackson through the darkness. Then Minton turned away from him and he felt as though his arms had been released; it was only at that moment that he realized that Minton had not laid a hand on him throughout their exchanges. He said, 'I – I'm not proud of what I did with Debbie. At the time when she was attending the youth club, I mean. But I didn't kill her. Perhaps I should have been of more help to her on that last Friday night, but I didn't know – '

'All right. You can go.' There was no pretence that this had been a meeting between equals, no attempt to disguise the fact that Minton had summoned the man here against his will. Suddenly, he was anxious only to be rid of this pathetic creature.

The vicar had parked in the anonymous wastes of the multi-storey. He wanted to leave this place of humiliation immediately, to drive swiftly to the relative safety of the high old vicarage rooms and the wife who knew of his weaknesses and had grown used to offering him her own strength. But his hands shook as he put them upon the steering wheel. He started the engine, and felt a welcome warmth stealing presently over the ageing upholstery. It was a full ten minutes before he trusted himself to ease the car down the concrete ramps to the exit.

He drove past Derek Minton's Astra as he went, but he did not register the man who had lately been his tormentor. Minton felt perfectly in control. He was merely composing himself, allowing the excitement to ooze away before he went back to a wife who must think he had been having a quiet drink in the warmth of the North Lancashire Golf Club.

He was a law-abiding man, who had never been in trouble with the police in his life. But if you were to secure the results you wanted, it was sometimes necessary to take the law into your own hands.

CHAPTER SIXTEEN

Superintendent Tommy Tucker was enjoying the media briefing he had arranged to update journalists and broadcasters about the investigations into the murder of Debbie Minton.

He had had his hair cut for the occasion (some of his colleagues said tinted and re-styled, but they were scarcely dispassionate observers). In his neatly pressed suit, with his striped tie and the immaculate shirt cuffs which he fingered from time to time, he presented the right police image of smartness and competence. He was sure of it.

And the questions he faced after his opening statement were scarcely demanding. A single Granada TV camera was there, but nothing from the BBC. The local press and Radio Lancashire were keen enough to hear him, though they knew him well enough to expect nothing very startling. The national papers' crime correspondents were mostly absent, content to rely on hearsay. Since the melodramatic activities of Frederick West in and around Gloucester, single killings of young women, even with the whiff of sex which always doubled the column inches, did not generate the excitement they once had.

There had been some lurid headlines and some splendid initial pictures of the newly blasted quarry pond where the remains of Debbie Minton had been found. But ten days later the story had run out of steam as far as the nationals were concerned. Of course, if the man proved obliging enough to go on to other mysterious killings; if he should turn himself into a serial killer, terrorizing even the sensible women of Lancashire . . .

But this killing had been two years ago, apparently, and the murderer had refused to add to his list of bodies in the intervening period. An audience of media people who felt they had supped full with horrors found it difficult to be excited by Superintendent Tucker's efforts, though they listened attentively enough, just in case.

'I can assure you that this case has top priority,' said Tucker impressively. As it was the only murder currently under investigation in Brunton, that was no more than routine procedure. 'I am happy to be able to tell you that my team has already made impressive progress.'

'What progress?' A man on the front row stopped picking his nose to make this abrupt interjection. He had not bothered to make a note throughout the account Tucker had just delivered to his audience. Tommy decided when he addressed himself to this disruption that he preferred his listeners to be young and dutiful. This man was neither. With his too-long grey hair and his nicotine-stained fingers, he was probably a hack who had been diverted from other pursuits to cover this briefing, just in case it produced anything new or unexpected.

Tucker turned for the first time to Percy Peach, who was sitting beside him and had been pointedly studying his beautifully manicured fingernails for the preceding five minutes. 'I think I'd like Detective Inspector Peach, one of my most valued and experienced officers, to take that one,' he said.

Percy looked briefly at Tucker, then with a not uncongenial distaste at the slumped figure on the front row of the scanty audience. 'We're making progress,' he said. 'Most of it I wouldn't care to report at the moment, except of course to my superior officers. This isn't the place for it, Bert.'

The man recognized the game they were engaged in. Despite himself, he was a little flattered to be recognized, to be treated by Peach as an old adversary, though they had spoken to each other only once before. He said, 'Does that in fact mean you've made no real progress at all?' Then, warming to the task, he grinned up at the platform and adopted his headline voice. ' "Local police baffled by ruthless killer." "Will this poor girl ever be avenged?" "Town waits with bated breath for sex killer's next strike." "Psychopath's cunning defies the local plod." ' He spread his gaze to take in all the policemen on the platform for his most daring sally. 'Is it perhaps time to get in help from elsewhere, I have to ask myself.'

Tucker sucked in his breath and prepared to be outraged, to denounce this irresponsible insolence. Percy, who recognized the technique of provoking a reaction by aggression because he used it so often himself, was merely amused. With his erect posture, short legs tucked under his chair as he leaned forward, his sprucely groomed air of shining cleanliness, Peach was a physical contrast to his slumped and raddled questioner, upon whom he now visited his brilliant beaver grin. 'Even you will understand, Bert, that there isn't much of a corpse left after two years at the bottom of a pond. You wouldn't expect forensic to be as helpful as usual, and they haven't been. But the diligent police work you choose to deride has been surprisingly successful. We have eliminated some twenty possible candidates – what you would no doubt call "suspects" – from our investigation. The public, I am happy to say, have been most helpful. We have several other people – I am not prepared to give you a number, of course – who are still helping us with our inquiries.'

'Useful phrase, that.' The journalist managed a sneer, but he was wishing he hadn't started this. When he had allowed himself to be irritated by that smug superintendent, he hadn't expected to be savaged by this bull terrier of an inspector.

'Very useful,' said Percy. 'Occasionally, as in this case, it is the only accurate summary we can release of what is going on.'

'Are you saying you are near to an arrest?' Bert was not a regular crime reporter, but he was an experienced hack, and he knew how to phrase an embarrassing question. The police wouldn't dare to say yes to that one, and if they said no, it made them sound like incompetent blunderers.

Percy Peach felt Tommy Bloody Tucker stirring uneasily on his right, preparing to come in with some emollient phrase, and it made him more direct than he might have been otherwise. 'I'm saying that we've made remarkable progress in the last week. That I expect to make an arrest for this crime within the next one.'

He was conscious of the little rumble of excitement among the hitherto docile audience but he did not take his eyes off the disconcerted, ageing face in the front row. There were a few more questions, but he explained that of course he could not reveal any more details. Not, as Superintendent Tucker came back belatedly into the exchanges to tell them, at this very delicate stage of the investigation.

Once Peach went back to inspecting his fingernails, the audience recognized that the newsworthy section of the briefing was over. Tommy Tucker assured them solemnly that he 'had taken personal charge of the investigation of this awful crime' and 'was determined to see it through to a successful conclusion.'

The meeting had already begun to break up.

Once the reporters and cameramen had been disposed of, Tucker peeled away his media smile and snapped, 'My office, Inspector Peach.'

Percy followed him with a carefully assumed air of innocent expectation. He always enjoyed a bollocking from Tommy Bloody Tucker.

'Were you lying out there?' said the superintendent. His anger made him handle Peach less cautiously than he normally did. He positively bristled.

'Oh no, sir. I don't believe in deceiving the public, even

when they are represented by people like Bert Allcock. Wonderful name for a tabloid scribe, don't you think, sir?'

'Why the hell wasn't I told? Didn't I direct you to keep me informed about all developments? Especially when there was a media conference this morning. You nearly made me look a fool out there.'

Percy reflected that Tommy needed no assistance in that. He said, 'I didn't know there was a conference until I arrived here this morning, sir. I didn't get the chance to speak to you before it because I was told by your secretary that you were closeted with the television make-up girls.'

Tucker glared at him, seeking for any sign of insolence in that round face. There was none: Peach's dark eyes might have been a fraction wider than usual, but that was all. The superintendent said, 'That's not bloody good enough, Peach, and you know it. You could have briefed me yesterday.'

'Had I known that we had this little exchange with the fourth estate planned for this morning, I should certainly have done that, sir. But my detective sergeant and I were pursuing our inquiries well into yesterday evening. It was after nine, indeed, when we arrived back in Brunton. Had I thought you would be at the station, I should certainly have come here, even at that hour. Were you here, sir?'

Tucker had left at five o'clock, as always, and they both knew it. He said, 'There was nothing to stop you ringing me at home. I'm always available, as you know, if there is urgent news about an investigation.'

Both of them knew that he never answered the phone, preferring to use his wife as a filter for his calls, declaring himself unavailable to all except his superior officers. Peach took his time, managing with a little difficulty to look contrite, hoping Tucker would congratulate himself on scoring a point. There was no hurry, when you had the boss trump still to play.

Presently he said, measuring his words with a slight air of puzzlement, as if still not quite sure where he had gone wrong, 'Yes, you've told me that before, sir. That's why I was bold enough to ring you last night, even at eleven o'clock. I wouldn't have dared to trouble any other senior officer but we all know here how conscientious you are, sir. You had your answering machine on, if you remember. I left a message saying I had news for you. Quite expected you to ring me back early this morning, as a matter of fact, but I expect you were busy with other things.'

Tucker knew exactly what was implied: he had been far too preoccupied with his preparations for the media conference to pay attention to his answerphone. He looked at his DI for a smouldering moment, during which Peach found the files on his desk of absorbing interest. Then he said, 'You'd better brief me now.'

Peach took him through a shortened version of the discussion he had conducted with Lucy Blake in the pub on the previous evening. There appeared now to be five main suspects, he explained, with the air of a man simplifying complex issues for a backward child. In his own mind, there were six, but he was not going to tell the establishment about Bob Cook until he was more certain about the degree of his involvement. 'Five, if you include Christine Turner as a separate suspect from her son, as I'm afraid we must,' he said firmly to his resentful superintendent.

'It won't be her,' said Tucker. 'Pillar of the community, she is.' Then, as Percy wondered if her husband had been a member of the lodge, Tucker said suddenly, as if the thought immediately exonerated her from all suspicion, 'Isn't she the Lady Captain at the North Lancs?'

'Ladies' Captain, we call it there, sir,' said Peach patiently. 'And even that office doesn't put her in the clear, in these democratic criminal days. She is also a mother, and mothers can be fierce in defence of their children, as I'm sure you know, sir.' Tucker had once failed to appear to support Peach at a promotions board because his wife insisted he attend his son's school sports day, and neither of them had forgotten it. Percy was convinced he would not have become an inspector without this absence; it was probably the one thing on which his superintendent agreed with him.

Tucker's brain sifted through the other names. With the air of a man offering a priceless insight from years of experience, he said, 'My money's on the black boy.'

'Gary Jones, sir. The lad on the greenkeeping staff at the North Lancs.' He had only just said the name, but he repeated it, as though it was important to check that a geriatric had fastened upon the right person.

'That's the one. He's got the background for crime. Probably a chip on his shoulder as well. You mark my words, when this is over, it'll be him we're banging up for this one.'

'That's a very interesting thought, sir. A hunch, I suppose you'd call it. You're well respected for them in the CID section, I know.' Peach's face had as much thought and expression as a ventriloquist's dummy's. At that moment, he found himself hoping against hope that Gary Jones was totally innocent. Tommy Bloody Tucker's view might be the first bit of luck the lad had had since the discovery of the little that was left of Debbie Minton.

Tucker's face brightened. The bollocking seemed to have gone wrong as usual but there was still the rare prospect of fun to be enjoyed at this awful man's expense. 'Getting on all right with your new detective sergeant, are you, Percy?'

For a moment, Peach allowed himself to look puzzled, whilst the expectation built in Tucker's battered breast. Then a smile lightened the inspector's stubby features. 'DS Blake, sir? Very promising CID officer, I think. Been a real help to me already. If I may say so, sir, I detect your hand in this appointment. You've always been such a good judge of men and their potential. And now of women. No one could accuse Superintendent Tucker of not moving with the times, eh, sir?'

Tucker's jaw had dropped at the beginning of this and

sunk further than seemed possible during its development, though Peach had affected not to notice it. The superintendent now seemed to have difficulty in getting his parted lips to meet again. Eventually he said, 'You – you haven't found it difficult at all? Er, working with a woman, I mean?'

'Not at all, sir. It's been a revelation. Between you and me, I said to myself, "If Thomas Tucker thinks she's got what it takes, then she must have. It's up to me to offer her every help I can, until she finds her own feet," I said. And I must say, that hasn't taken her long. Lucy – sorry, I suppose I should say DS Blake, but we've got used to working without the formalities – has settled in very quickly. I already find it difficult to remember how I operated without her. Not that I've anything against DS Collins, you understand, but sometimes personalities just go well together. I expect you spotted that possibility, sir. I know how much thought you put into building up the right team.'

'But you're a – you're a traditionalist, Percy. You can't enjoy working with a woman, surely? Not from what I've seen of you before.'

'Never let it be said that Percy Peach isn't open to new ideas, sir. You've taught me that, I often feel. We have to move with the times. I remember you saying that when some of us had reservations. And how right you've been.'

'You haven't found Sergeant Blake – well, a bit too forthright and independent in her views?'

'Oh, no, sir. I like to think I keep abreast of the leading thinkers like yourself, in my quiet way. Still too many chauvinists in the police, in my view. But things are changing all the time. I'm sure our own CID section can thank your enlightened leadership for much of that. And there's no doubt you've given me a gem in Lucy Blake. A gem, sir.'

'You haven't found her gender has got in the way of good detection, then? I know you had some reservations when – '

'Me, sir? Reservations? I must have given the wrong impression – but then I haven't your communication skills.

Or your vision. Just a villain-taker: I know that's my reputation, and I can't deny it. But Lucy Blake has given a new perspective to my work. More flexible, we are, as a duo. She has skills I couldn't offer. And she seems to respect my experience, I'm glad to say. I can't really envisage a more effective combination.'

He beamed his dazzling beaver beam at Thomas Tucker and dismissed himself.

Peach did not have to seek out Bob Cook. The young constable rang in from Preston and asked to see him.

'I'll come to your house,' said Percy with cheerful malevolence.

'No, not there!' said Cook hastily. 'I'll come and see you at Brunton CID; I finish my shift in an hour. It needs to be private. But it shouldn't take more than a few minutes.'

'Let's hope it doesn't, lad,' muttered Peach to the phone after he had set it down. He was only thirty-six, but he had been in the force for eighteen years. Policemen who turned to crime were the dregs, dragging down the reputation of every copper in the country along with them. If Cook was among them, he would receive no mercy from Percy Peach.

Cook was still in uniform when he arrived in Brunton CID. Perhaps he hoped that the curious would take it that he was merely reporting in on a routine criminal matter. Being in the uniformed branch, he had never worked with Peach in CID. Though occasional police-lore snippets of Peach's fearsome approach to petty criminals had seeped through to him, he had hitherto known Percy only as an indifferent golfer.

Such experience can colour a man's thoughts and leave him unready for the exchanges of real life.

Bob Cook found a woman with Peach. She was business-like in full-sleeved green blouse and tartan skirt; as he entered, he felt himself assessed by the bright blue-green eyes beneath the wide forehead with its frame of dark red hair. His first thought was that she was a secretary. It was briskly dismissed by Peach. 'Detective Sergeant Lucy Blake, Constable Bob Cook. Sit yourselves down and let's get going.'

Cook stood awkwardly before the proffered chair. Lucy Blake had nodded and smiled at him, but he took his eyes from her, not wishing to seem insulting in what he had to say. 'I said on the phone that what I had to say was private, Percy. Just between the two of us.'

'And I said when you rang that I was going to contact you in any case. DS Blake is here in her professional capacity, at my request. Unless I decide that what you have to say is unconnected with any criminal matter, she stays here.'

Cook became very stiff. 'In that case, sir, I have made a mistake. I came here voluntarily. If we cannot speak alone, I feel there is no purpose in a meeting.'

'Please yourself, Bob. But you're involved in the Debbie Minton murder case. We shall be investigating you anyway.'

'What do you mean "involved"? I've no connection with that wretched girl's death.' He could not summon up the tone he wanted, so that what he meant as outrage emerged almost as apology. He needed suddenly to sit down, as he felt his senses racing, but to do so seemed to admit the very association he was denying.

'Maybe not. But you applied for a transfer on your first working day after the girl's death, and chose not to reveal that to me. I was bound to find that interesting, coming as it did from a policeman who knows we're involved in the investigation of a murder. DS Blake, incidentally, already knows about this. We await your explanation of your actions with interest.'

Now Cook did sit down. He was a young, fit man, but as he felt the dizzying impact of Peach at his most inexorable he needed a chair. He could not rid his mind of the irrelevant notion that he should never have proposed this man for membership of the golf club, as if Peach's new proximity

to the place where the body had been discovered had somehow sharpened his awareness of the issues. Cook managed
to say dully, 'I didn't strangle Debbie Minton.'

'I'm glad to hear it. Now convince us.'

Bob Cook glared at him in outrage. Logic told him that
it was silly to count on their fellowship as golfers for anything, but they were also fellow-policemen. Surely that
meant something? Peach's answer was to study him as
dispassionately as if he were a rat involved in some scientific experiment, whose reactions might now be of great
research value.

It was Lucy Blake who said, 'This is a murder investigation, Bob. You can gain nothing by trying to deceive us. You
must realize that it can only be a matter of time before we
dig out whatever it is you would like to conceal.'

She was younger than he was, and his first male response
was to reject her soft-voiced counsel as presumptuous. But
he knew enough about the resources which went into a
murder investigation to realize that what she said was no
less than the truth. He did not look at her but he said to the
implacable Peach, 'What is it you want to know?'

'We need to know all about your relationship with Debbie
Minton. Everything. With dates, as far as possible.'

Cook looked at the squat features with undisguised hostility. He had come here voluntarily, and run into this barrage.
But he knew deep within him that he had merely been
hoping to spike some CID guns by his voluntary presence,
perhaps even to gain some kudos through giving information on his own terms. Now these terms had been rejected
and new ones dictated. That was what he was resentful
about, even though he realized only dimly what had happened. He said sullenly, 'I had a relationship with Debbie.
Over about a year.'

'Which was the year before she disappeared?'

'Yes.'

'And how far did this relationship extend?' Peach saw the

desperation creeping across the harassed face. Before Cook could attempt the prevarication which would invite a further mauling, he said, 'You were knocking her off, weren't you, Bob?'

Cook glanced involuntarily at Lucy Blake, embarrassed by Peach's earthiness, wishing again that they could have done this without her here. He had not thought himself a conventional man until now. He said helplessly, 'Yes. I'm not proud of it.'

'I hope not.' Peach paused, studying the now abject figure in the armchair beyond his desk. He was like a prizefighter, deciding that a few vigorous blows to the body now might set up the knock-out to conclude the contest. 'You're a married man with two children, Bob. What is the state of your marriage?'

'It – it's okay. I don't see that it's relevant to this.'

'Don't you? Was there ever a question of your leaving your wife?'

'No!' Cook was aghast at the suggestion, and his denial came almost before the question was concluded.

'So Debbie was no more than a bit on the side.'

Cook hesitated, searching desperately for a way round the sordid suggestion, failing to find one. 'I suppose so. It didn't feel like that at the time.'

'You're not the first man to take what he can get. But this was after you'd questioned her about her involvement with drugs, wasn't it?'

It was an educated guess, which hit the mark. Cook nodded miserably.

'So you were exploiting a professional relationship. A young girl was grateful for getting off with a warning about the drugs and you stepped in and got her drawers down while she was still being grateful.' As Cook made to protest, he said sharply, 'That's how a barrister would put it, if it suited him. You've been to court often enough to know the score.'

'I suppose so. But I didn't see it like that. I'm not denying that I should have done.'

Peach sighed. 'This isn't a moral investigation. For what it's worth to your career and your marriage, no one outside this room knows about this meeting. If you prove to have had nothing to do with this death, I'll try to keep it like that, but there are no promises. This is a murder investigation, and we'll probe everything connected with the victim.'

While Cook looked as if he were struggling towards some kind of thanks, Lucy Blake said, 'There were other people getting what they wanted from Debbie Minton, as well as you. Sex, to put it in a word.' She waited to see if he would claim his relationship was different, which might have been significant. When he did not, she said, 'Did you know she was promiscuous?'

He looked at her serious young face, with its freckles and its earnest openness. At that moment, he hated her, for her youth and her rank. He said, 'At the time, I don't think I did. Perhaps I chose to ignore what was there for me to see.' His self-disgust was suddenly manifest.

'Were you still seeing her at the time of her disappearance?'

If he knew how vital a question it was, he gave no sign. 'No. We'd packed it in not long before.' Then, as if remembering that he was a policeman and mindful of Peach's reminder about dates, he said, 'About a month before, I suppose. Maybe a little less.'

Lucy said, 'When you say, "We'd packed it in", do you mean it was a mutual decision? Or merely that you had decided that enough was enough as far as you were concerned?'

'It – it was me. I realized that Debbie wasn't reliable. She was quite wild in what she said, sometimes. I was afraid it would get back to Sue.' He was shamefaced now, surprised to find the woman so calm in her questioning.

'But you knew she was pregnant.'

She fed in the key question as a statement, implying that they knew far more than they did, and it worked. 'Yes.'

'Were you the father?'

There was a silence, when they had least expected it. For a moment, she thought she was going to have to put the question again. Then he said slowly, 'No. I'm sure I wasn't. But Debbie said I was.' He looked up at them, his wide, suddenly naive, eyes full of puzzlement. 'I could never quite be sure when that girl was being serious. She was threatening to tell everything to Sue.'

CHAPTER SEVENTEEN

Gary Jones was terrified that the police would search his room. He had been brought up to distrust them, and he did not understand the law about search warrants. He had learned over the years that a black boy who was under suspicion didn't get much joy from quoting the rule-book.

He should have got rid of Debbie Minton's brooch. He knew that. He did not need a river, though the Ribble was within three miles of where he worked. He crossed the Leeds and Liverpool canal every day on his way from the grubby Brunton street where he lived to the golf club. He began work at seven, even in the winter months, so that there was no one about when he crossed the old stone bridge beneath which the sweating horses had once tugged the coal-filled barges.

It would have been simple to brake the little Honda motor-cycle and toss the brooch into the filthy grey water beneath him; he needn't even have dismounted. But he could not bring himself to throw away his last link with Debbie. Instead, he took the brooch, wrapped in a clean handkerchief, and put it at the back of the single shelf in his locker in the greenkeepers' shed. In the months to come, he would ask himself many times how he could have been so foolish. He knew the answer, though at first he did not care to admit it to himself: he was still not rid of Debbie Minton. The hold he thought he had broken two years earlier was upon him still.

For three days, he left the little package undisturbed. Then, in the gloom of the late afternoon when the others had left, he saw the white cotton wrapping, startlingly obvious when everything else in his locker was indistinct. He looked at it for a few seconds, telling himself it was time to change his shoes and be off.

Then, like an ex-smoker asserting that he was strong enough now to hold the cigarette packet in his reformed hands, he reached in and took out the brooch.

The pewter was dull, scarcely visible in the subdued light at this darkest corner of the huge, concrete-walled shed. But the fragments of green glass gleamed bright as the emeralds they simulated, bringing back memories of a laughing girl, flinging back her dark hair, thrusting the new brooch she was so proud of close to his dark eyes, which could focus only on the soft breast which was so desirable beneath it.

'Pretty, that.'

Gary's heart leapt so fiercely that he felt for a moment as if his whole body had left the floor. His head swam as he turned, so that he had to clutch at the open door of the metal locker to retain his balance.

Charlie Booth. Grinning like a devil discovering sin, holding in his hand the billhook he had been using to clear a wooded bank on the course. The years dropped away and Gary was back in the playground, a skinny black boy in short trousers, confronting a stocky, grinning figure who had called him nigger and thrown a banana skin in his face.

The fight had ranged over three corners of the old concrete playground, then out on to the edge of the grimy winter playing field. He had beaten the bigger boy in the end, against all the odds, though no one except the watchers could have discerned from their bloodied noses and grazed knees who had been the victor. But he had been on top, raining blows from his small fists upon the writhing heap beneath him, when the master had finally arrived. Every one of the pupils who had ringed the flailing limbs to urge on this eruption of boyish hatreds knew who had won.

Neither of them had mentioned the fight from that day to this, through five years of the comprehensive and two years of working together at the North Lancs. But the resentment had lain between them like a shrouded corpse, silent but unforgettable. Suddenly, the corpse was rearing itself into life.

Charlie Booth moved forward, savouring his advantage, taking the brooch from the palsied fingers which closed too late in defence. 'Very pretty indeed.' He looked at Gary's face, then back at the bauble in his grubby palm, recognition dawning. In that moment, fear mixed itself with the delight on the flat, revealing features. He said, 'This is Debbie Minton's, isn't it? We all knew you were daft about the bitch.'

'Give it back!' Gary grasped at it, remembering how Debbie had rejected Booth for him, and how delighted he had been by that at the time.

'Not likely!' Charlie was back in the playground again all those years ago, taunting the wide-eyed black face with the single-minded malevolence of a child, turning sideways to keep his burly torso between the grasping fingers and his trophy. His shirt was open to the waist with the effort of using the billhook on the course. Gary could smell the sweat, mingling with the blood from the shallow bramble scratches on his tormentor's body as they struggled over the brooch.

Then, without warning, Booth was overtaken by the considerations of an adult. 'How do you come to have this? Was she wearing this when − ?' He thrust the trophy away from him as eagerly as he had grasped it, back into the hands which had sought it in vain a moment earlier. 'No wonder you were worried when they said we were going to drain the old quarry pond. You knew she was in there! You knew because you'd put her there.'

Charlie Booth backed away as he said it, raising the billhook he had been using on the course, a medieval serf prepared to defend himself from a violent contemporary. He kept his eyes on Gary Jones until he reached the door, then flung the weapon away as he turned and ran.

The master should have come earlier to save him all those years ago in the playground. This time he would find the master for himself. Gary watched the flying figure hopelessly from the door of the shed, as it raced towards the clubhouse and the secretary's office.

When you were in trouble, you turned back to your parents. You liked to pretend you were fully independent, even to make gentle fun of the old worriers when you talked to your fellow-students, but you were glad they were there when you needed them. When you only had one parent, she was even more vital to you in times of stress. You did not admit it, of course, or even say where you were going. But you went, nevertheless.

Francis Turner went home to consult his mother.

Or rather, not quite home, but to her office at Turner Home Services. It felt a little less like running back to mother to go there; he could pretend to be taking an interest in the business which his father had founded and his mother now ran: the family business, though none of them had ever described it as that.

Perhaps there was a tiny concession to the idea of proprietorship in his dress. He adhered to the student uniform of jeans and sweatshirt, but they were his newest ones, and they were immaculately clean. The big one-storey building with its long counter was as busy as ever, so that the staff who spoke to him as he passed had scarcely time to notice his dress.

Christine Turner rose as if he had been a customer as he went into her neat office. For a moment, there was a little awkwardness between them, which there would not have been in the privacy of their home. It was not helped by the reason for this meeting; anxiety hung in the air between them in the instant before he hugged her against his slim chest.

How vulnerable he seemed to her! So tall now, and yet still a child! She could feel his heart pounding against the side of her head as she rested it against him, not wanting to break the moment with the words she knew must come. But even as she broke away from him, she heard herself saying, 'Well? What did they have to say?'

'Easy, Mum, easy!' He guided her gently to the armchair, then sat opposite her. But they were each on the edge of their chairs, sitting upright, scarcely three feet from each other. Like conspirators, he thought.

'You first!' he grinned, trying to lighten the tension he felt between them. He had never felt it before, not quite like this. Any experienced CID man would have recognized the stress which spreads out from a murder investigation to all those involved in it.

'I told you. The woman came to see me. Detective sergeant, I think she is. Perhaps I shouldn't have, but I quite liked her. I told her about Debbie in the time she spent here. About the disruption she caused. "An easy screw", one of the men called her: that about summed it up.' Christine could not prevent her old resentment that her son should have fallen for such a creature from tumbling out.

'Did you tell Detective Sergeant Blake that?' Francis Turner had always been able to remember names; his older relations found it one of his more annoying traits.

'Yes, if that was her name.' She saw her son's disappointment in her. 'Debbie Minton caused me far too much trouble, here and elsewhere, for me to want to protect her reputation, Francis.'

'Me being the elsewhere.' For a moment they were on the verge of quarrelling, of renewing the old high words of two years and more ago. Then he said, 'I'm sorry. You've every right to resent her, even now. I suppose I was just trying to take my share of the blame.'

She reached out and took his hand, her irritation transformed in an instant into a mother's protectiveness. 'Don't talk like that, please, love. Not now. I didn't mention you to the policewoman, and she didn't press me.'

Francis smiled grimly. 'Well, they pressed me. Your Sergeant Blake and that rottweiler of an inspector who seems to be in charge.'

'Percy Peach.' This time it was she who was surprised by her recall of the name. She smiled as she explained it. 'He's a member of the golf club. A new one. But he didn't come here.'

'Perhaps he didn't fancy bearding the Ladies' Captain in her den. Anyway, he took it out on me.'

'They knew about you?'

'Of course they did.' For a moment, he was irritated by her innocence. 'They knew all about Debbie and me dabbling with the drugs. They have their records, even though we weren't charged. And you might just as well have mentioned me – no doubt it only made them more suspicious when you didn't. They've been talking to everyone who went about with Debbie in the period before she disappeared, as you might expect.'

Christine Turner felt suddenly desperate. Was it all to go wrong, in the end? Were all her unaccustomed deceits to be for nothing? She said, trying to keep a note of apology out of her voice, 'I told them about Debbie and the drugs. I just didn't mention you.'

'That was probably a mistake.' He said it with a casual, unthinking cruelty. 'They realized how worried you were about my relationship with Debbie, anyway.'

'How much did you tell them?' Fearing the answer so much, she had to force herself to ask the question.

For the first time, he registered the suffering on her face. 'I told them you'd warned me against her, but I wouldn't listen. I told them she was opening her legs to all and sundry.' It was the first time he had used a phrase like that with his mother, and he looked up at her automatically to see if it had shocked her.

Her only reaction was a worried nod. 'What about the pregnancy?'

'They asked me if I knew about it when she disappeared. I said yes. I didn't want them catching me out in lies, and I wasn't sure how much they knew. They were clever about that.'

'And no doubt they wanted to know if you were the father.'

'Yes. I told them I didn't know. I didn't think I was, but I could have been, I said.'

'Oh, Francis! They'll think whoever was the father of that foetus is their killer. I'm sure of it.'

'Well, I thought it best to tell them the truth, as far as possible.' He smiled at her, a boy again, wanting to be praised as he always had been for his honesty, little realizing how much it had cost her to try her clumsy, ineffective deceptions on his behalf. 'Anyway, I held back the important bit. I didn't tell them how we'd tried to buy her off. How she'd refused to allow us to pay for an abortion.'

'We've been talking to some of the members of your youth club, Joe.' Peach stretched his short legs in front of him. The Reverend Joseph Jackson was regretting asking to be addressed as Joe at their first meeting. It seemed much more than a few days ago. But a lot had happened since then. And this awful man with the taunting beaver grin was going on. 'Not to your present clientele, of course, Joe. We've spoken to the ones who were the contemporaries of Debbie Minton.'

'I see. Of course, one loses touch with most of them, unless they come regularly to church. And regrettably – '

'They've been very helpful to us, those boys and girls. Men and women now, I should say, of course. Reliable witnesses if we should need them in court, I should think – forgive me, Joe, but we policemen tend to think in these terms, I'm afraid.' Again there came that awful grin, leering at Jackson like a Cheshire cat from between the wings of the old high-backed armchair in the vicarage reception room.

The vicar licked his lips, looking hopefully at Lucy Blake, but finding no salvation in that young and serious face. 'Were they able to help you at all? With finding out who killed Debbie Minton, I mean?'

'They were very helpful. Very co-operative, even the ones who didn't like the police, once we'd shown them what was what.'

'That's good.'

'Isn't it? It's gratifying to find the young so helpful. They told us Debbie was sleeping around. "Putting it about a bit" was the phrase most of them used, I think. Not a very pleasing term, but vivid, in its way, I suppose. But then you'd already told us much the same thing, Joe, so they were merely confirming it for us.'

'Did they – did they come up with anything else that was useful?' Jackson wondered why he was drawn on, in spite of himself. Peach seemed to expect it of him, and he was no match for this man's will.

'Yes, they did, Joe. That's why we're here, as a matter of fact. But then, I expect you've deduced that for yourself. We CID people sometimes think we have a monopoly, whereas any intelligent person like yourself can make deductions, of course.' He smiled contentedly, enjoying this philosophical strain. 'I suppose what distinguishes us professionals is that we have some experience to draw on; and of course we are in a position to put together all the findings from different sources. That sometimes makes us look rather cleverer than we are, fortunately. For instance, I can now confirm that we are definitely interested in the older man Debbie was associating with.'

'Or men.' Jackson was pleased with this, but he could not manage the self-deprecating smile he tried to produce.

'Or men, as you say. Things are never straightforward in

this life, are they? But several of these young people have told us the same thing about one older person, and that is quite useful to us. But not to you, I'm afraid: rather the opposite, in fact.'

'I – I'm afraid I don't quite understand. I told you everything I could last time you – '

'Hands up skirts, Joe. Very naughty. Especially for a vicar, most people would say. Position of trust, and all that.'

'Now look here – '

'No, you look, Joe!' Peach's voice was suddenly like a whiplash. 'We've quite enough to put you in court, if we need to. And Debbie Minton was under sixteen at the time of the first offence. Jail bait. And you must have known it.'

'I didn't have sex with her. I was weak, I don't deny it, but she led me on. I wish I'd never seen her.' Jackson thrust his face into his hands as his voice croaked out the sentiment they had heard so often. Then his shoulders were wracked by tearless sobbing: they could scarcely hear his muffled voice as he brought out the phrase he had rehearsed over the long nights of anticipation of this moment. 'There was no penetration, you know.'

Peach nodded at Lucy Blake, and she said, 'Perhaps not, Mr Jackson, but there would be a charge of indecent assault, at the very least.' The wretched figure opposite them nodded, head still clutched in the large hands. 'We can't guarantee that there will be no such a charge, but we won't be instrumental in bringing it. We're interested in the greater crime of murder, you see. If you can help us with that, it is bound to help you.' She did not know if she should have gone so far, but Peach seemed to approve it.

Percy said to the cringing figure, 'Help you, that is.. Unless you killed her, of course. Did you kill her, Joe?'

Jackson felt so weary of the nightmare that he had scarcely the energy to deny them. They were going to get him, anyway, despite what the girl had said. And if they didn't there was always the dead girl's father. You couldn't expect mercy from him. Almost half a minute passed before he said, 'I didn't kill Debbie Minton. I didn't even have sex with her. I touched her. And she touched me. A few times. And she was probably under sixteen, at first, as you say. It was just a bit of cheap excitement, for her. When I saw the way she went on with others afterwards, I was sure of that. It didn't even seem such a big thing at the time – I'm sure it wasn't to her. But it's haunted me ever since. And now it's going to destroy me.'

The words came abruptly, between breaths he could not control. He had abandoned all thought of the phrases he had rehearsed so often for this dreaded moment. They listened to his horrid breathing for another long thirty seconds, wondering if he had more confessions, more revelations for them. Then Lucy Blake said gently, 'Did you have any association with her in the months before she died, Mr Jackson?'

The carefully chosen phrase hung in the air for a moment. When he spoke, his brow was furrowed in concentration, as if he was determined now that he would offer them no further deception. 'No. That was long past.'

Lucy said, 'Think carefully, please, because this is very important. Can you think of any man who had a close relationship with Debbie in those last weeks before she disappeared?'

'No. I've thought about it, as you can imagine. If I could, it would get me off the hook, wouldn't it?' His wide wet eyes held not hope but an appeal for some crumb of reassurance as he raised them for the first time in several minutes.

Peach said, 'It might. If you were telling the truth, of course. We have to make that reservation about everyone, Joe. Even for vicars with wandering hands: perhaps especially for them. Did you speak to Debbie Minton in those last weeks?'

'God help me, he knows!' thought Jackson. This bullying beaver of a man seemed to know everything. He said, 'I suppose you've got this from Derek Minton. Yes, she came to see me on the night she disappeared. But I didn't kill her!' His voice rose a little on this insistence but it seemed to him a hopeless denial now. His head dropped again, so that he did not see the looks his two interrogators exchanged.

'What did she come to see you about, Joe?'

'She came to ask me for advice.' Suddenly he giggled, as the ridiculous irony of that struck him. How on earth could he expect them to believe that? Well, he was beyond caring now whether they did or they didn't. 'She didn't say openly that she was pregnant but I guessed at it from other things she said. She said I was the only one she could trust.'

This time the giggle rose towards hysteria, and Peach wondered if he should slap the heavy, mobile features. Instead, he said sharply, 'Who was the father, Joe? Did she tell you?'

'No, she didn't even discuss it.'

'Then what did she want to talk about?'

'She said there was an older man. She wanted to get rid of him, but she didn't know how.'

'What was his name, Joe?'

'She didn't say. All she said was that she wanted to get rid of him, but she didn't know how to go about it.'

'Was he the man who had made her pregnant?'

'I don't know. I told you, we didn't even discuss it openly.'

'So what was your advice?'

'I'm afraid I wasn't much use. I told her to go and talk it over with her parents. She said she couldn't, but then young people always say that at first, don't they?' He looked up at them, seeking not approval – that was far too much – but some sort of agreement. 'I – I didn't know then that it would be the last time I spoke to her, did I?'

Again he looked into their alert, attentive faces, searching for the confirmation that did not come.

CHAPTER EIGHTEEN

Paul Capstick normally felt thoroughly in control in his secretary's office at the North Lancashire Golf Club. It was his domain, and he had the confidence that comes from knowing more about what goes on in a place than any other single person. Yet on this occasion he was nervous.

The man in front of him was a new member, who would normally have been diffident in this room, searching for guidance and reassurance. As a golfer, even DI Percy Peach might have been a little overawed by the panelled walls and the ancient sepia photographs of the secretary's office. But in his professional capacity, he was too preoccupied even to consider such a preposterous notion.

'Where is he?' he said.

'I've put him in the television room to wait for us. He's a good lad really, Percy. Been a good worker here. We were expecting him to do very well. He says he – '

'Better hear what he has to say for himself, I think. Let's have him in here right away.'

Gary Jones shuffled in like a condemned man, looking from his boss to Percy Peach and on to Lucy Blake. Then his gaze fixed upon the inspector's left hand, which held Debbie Minton's brooch.

'All right, lad. Don't waste our time. Where did you get it?'

'On the path near the quarry. The one on the eighth. Where – '

'Where the body of your former girlfriend was found. This is Debbie's, isn't it?'

'Yes. She was very proud of it.'

'When did you find it?'

'A long time ago.'

'You can do better than that, lad.'

'Two years. I found it early one Saturday morning, when I was the duty greenkeeper, out raking the bunkers.'

'The morning after Debbie disappeared.'

'Yes. I think it was, now. At the time, I didn't know that.'

'Why didn't you produce this when she became a missing person and the uniformed men were asking questions about her?'

The tortured features twitched a little, but remained silent for a long, agonized moment. The mind behind them was searching for words it had never needed before. 'She was only – only missing, then. I thought she'd gone away somewhere. The brooch was all I had left to remember her by.' It made more sense than he thought it did, but it came out unevenly, as he snatched at ideas before they could elude him.

'But you knew Debbie's body was in that pond, didn't you?'

Lucy Blake and Capstick looked at each other involuntarily. But Jones was too preoccupied to notice it. 'I didn't at first. But when she didn't turn up and no one heard anything from her, I began to think she must be in there, because of finding the brooch where I did. That's why I was upset when I heard about the quarry pond being blasted away to change the eighth hole.'

Peach looked at him for a moment, waiting to see if he would go any further. Then he said slowly, 'Were you scared because you *knew* she was in there, Gary? Knew because you had put her in that pond, keeping the brooch as a remembrance of the days you'd had together?' Peach's voice would normally have hectored his victim on such a suggestion. This time his tone was quiet, almost sympathetic. It was a strain Lucy Blake had never heard in him before.

'No. I didn't put her there. But I found the brooch within a few yards of that water, on what turned out to be the morning after she disappeared. I just became more and more certain as the months passed that someone had dumped her in there. I wanted to tell someone what I thought, but I thought I'd be suspected of killing her if I did.'

He was right, thought Peach. He would immediately have become the chief suspect, in those circumstances. Percy said almost gently, 'And who do you think killed her, lad?'

'I – I've no idea.' Jones wanted to go on, to explain how much he had thought about that question. But he was so suffused by relief that he could not do it. It seemed that this awful man, whom he had thought would seize the opportunity to lock him away, might actually believe him.

Peach studied the slim black figure for a moment longer, then spoke to Paul Capstick. 'Gary could do with a coffee, I think. Perhaps with a dash of something stronger in it. DS Blake and I must be off.' He turned back to Jones. 'I'll have to keep the brooch, lad. It's evidence now, you see; and you'll probably become a witness, in due course.'

They left secretary and junior greenkeeper, highest and lowest employees in the North Lancs hierarchy, looking equally bemused and relieved in the doorway of the office.

So it was to end where it had begun. In the car they talked in snatches, each thinking about what was to come, neither of them caring to voice their feelings about it. Lucy Blake drove slowly as the lane snaked over the moor, allowing them a distant view of Pen-y-Ghent and Ingleborough, forty miles to the north.

Peach said suddenly, 'We could become a good team, you and I. I told Tommy Tucker that.'

It was so far from what they had been a week ago that they both burst into laughter at the idea. Lucy said, 'I bet that pleased him. He only brought me in to annoy you, you know. He said I was to go to him if I had any trouble with you.'

'But you didn't.'

'Have trouble?'

'No, you daft cow. You didn't go to Tommy Bloody Tucker.'

'No. I prefer to solve my own problems, when I can.'

'I've noticed.'

'But Percy Peach is no problem. He's easy to work with when you know how.' On that first day, she would never have believed she would come to say such things. Daringly, she mimicked the uncertainty of his opening remark, 'I think we could become a good team, you and I.' Then she watched the road ahead with great concentration, though there was no traffic visible.

He grinned, then put out his hand to rest lightly on the smaller one that lay on the gear stick between them. 'You might have other problems with me, in due course.'

'I expect I shall be able to deal with those too, Inspector. Without recourse to Tommy Bloody Tucker.'

The house looked like all the others in the row, except that it was perhaps a little better maintained, a little more trimly presented in the morning sunshine. The grime of the town which was only two miles away was invisible from here. There was a glimpse of the shoulder of Pendle Hill behind the suburban neatness as one looked to the north.

It was Derek Minton who opened the front door to them, his face clear and untroubled. 'We can speak freely if you have any news for me,' he said as he led them indoors. 'Shirley has gone to the doctor's.'

They knew that. They had engineered that she would be detained there for longer than he thought. She was going to need some counselling. And much, much more than that.

They sat on the three-piece suite in the comfortable lounge, with the detectives each on the edge of an armchair and Minton sitting back on the settee, his arms stretched along the back of it, as though he was encouraging them to relax with him. He said, 'Are you any nearer to finding out who killed our Debbie? I appreciate that it must be difficult for you after all this time, but – '

'We know who killed her.' Peach was calm, watchful, very quiet even in that quiet room. Was it to be as low-key as this, Lucy wondered. It was her first murder case, her first arrest for that most ancient and most awful of crimes. She could see the two protagonists watching each other, still as lizards at this moment, Peach sitting very erect on her right, Minton still simulating relaxation on the sofa in front of her.

She watched him now lean forward, producing the right degree of animation in response to Peach's assertion. 'That's good, Inspector. I can't tell you how much of a relief it will be to both of us. Perhaps now we shall be able to start getting on with our lives again. I think Shirley is beginning to pick up the pieces a little at last . . .'

Peach had let him go on, amazed at the steadiness of his voice, curious to see how long it would be before he ran out of the platitudes he thought appropriate, studying him like a specimen newly arrived under a microscope. It was the mention of Shirley Minton that galvanized Peach. He moved quickly over the seven feet that separated him from Minton, who half rose as he came but offered no aggression. Peach pronounced the formal words of the caution with his hand lightly upon the shoulder of the wiry figure. It looked to Lucy Blake like a tableau which might have been frozen into a Victorian story painting, so quietly was the moment achieved by both the parties concerned in it.

Minton looked for an instant as if he would deny the charge and continue for a little while longer the charade of his innocence. Then he sank back on to the sofa and said, 'She was a nymphomaniac, you know, our Debbie. I suppose that's the word for it. I heard one of the lads say prick-teaser but it went further than that.'

Lucy Blake said, 'She enjoyed sex, anyway. We've been able to establish that.' She was not sure why she had spoken. She did not think it was to defend her sex against further spatterings, nor even to assert her presence in this meeting where she had not yet spoken. Probably it was to release her own tension: she felt a little of it drop away with her words.

Minton said, 'She enticed me into her bedroom, the first time. I didn't realize what was happening, until it was too late.'

It was the weak man's old excuse. But he sounded dispassionate, almost curious in his examination of how this awful thing had evolved. 'It was Debbie who said, "We aren't related by blood, you know, so it's all right between the two of us. It won't be incest." I should have known then that it would be disastrous. But she was an attractive girl. And I did love her, you know, when she was younger, in a different way. Like a daughter. What we did took me by surprise.'

Suddenly, his face was in his hands and he was sobbing quietly. The emotion came as a relief to them; it was much less disturbing than his previous emotionless account of the emerging tragedy.

After a moment, Peach said, 'How old was she when this happened?'

'Nineteen. The first time was four months before – before she disappeared.' Even now, he preferred to maintain that evasive phrase.

'And it became a regular thing between the two of you.'

'Yes. In the evenings, when Shirley was working at the supermarket. She was there on three nights a week, as I told you. She never suspected. But then, she had no idea what Debbie was like when it came to sex. Neither had I, at the start. I thought I was special.' His face set like stone on the last words. They had heard the same sentiment before about the dead girl, coming from others. The echo from this source had a chilling irony.

'But eventually you found out about her activities.' Peach was studiously neutral, a prompt towards further revelations from the quiet man on the sofa.

'Yes. A few things came back to me from people in the office. When I challenged her, she told me everything. I see now that she was besotted with sex. I was just something else to try.' He buried his face in his hands again. 'You won't believe me, but I love my Shirley. It was because I couldn't bear to lose her that I did this.'

Lucy Blake, busy recording his exact words now that he had been cautioned, wondered if this constituted a confession. She said, like a doctor taking a patient through the history of an illness, 'Was it the pregnancy that brought matters to a head?'

'Yes. She said I was the father. Now, I don't know whether I was or not, but I believed her at the time.'

'And you tried to get her to have an abortion.'

'Yes. She wouldn't go to the doctor, so I got the number of a private clinic for her. Even offered to arrange it all myself, but she wouldn't have that. I left the number with her, hoping she'd see sense, but she wouldn't make her mind up. Kept saying perhaps she ought to keep the child, and telling me her mother wouldn't approve of an abortion. I think now that she was quite enjoying the situation.'

'So you felt that you had to cut short the arguments.'

Minton paused, weighing up the situation as coolly as a man playing chess. Then he nodded, as composed as if he were explaining a committee decision in the council office. 'She was going to tell Shirley about what had been going on between us, and I couldn't have that.' He spoke as calmly as a father forbidding a daughter to be in late. It was difficult to believe that this self-possessed figure, sitting still but erect now on the sofa, was a murderer, who had maintained his secret for two years whilst ministering to the wife he still loved.

It was Peach who said quietly, carefully maintaining his neutral tone, 'So you killed her, Derek.'

Minton registered no surprise at this first use of his forename; perhaps he did not even notice it. 'Yes. I had to.

She mocked me when I said her mother must know nothing about us. She said I was no more proof than all the other men against the attractions of young flesh, and that Shirley had better know about that. Perhaps she wasn't serious: I could never tell as she got wilder what she really meant to do.'

It was on that thought that his voice faltered for the first and only time. At that moment they were sorry for him, as the scene in that quiet house sprang vividly alive for them. They could see the laughing girl, unconscious of her danger, and the desperate man who was losing the power of reason in the face of her derision. Then Peach said harshly, 'So you strangled her. Was it here?'

'Yes. In this very room.' He looked beside him at the sofa, as if he sought confirmation from some invisible presence, and they knew suddenly that it had been there that Debbie Minton had died, bending back over the top of the couch as those steely fingers ground ruthlessly into her slim neck.

'And you knew how to dispose of the body.'

'Yes. It was as though I had planned it all, though I don't think I had. It was half past seven on an October evening. I knew there would be no one around in the darkness if I took her up to the old quarry on the golf course. I'd often thought when I played my golf that a body could lie undiscovered for ever in that pond. I never thought it would be me who tested the theory.'

Minton was back in his analytical vein, explaining the detail of murder as if it had been no more than a planning problem in his local government department. He looked up at Peach without rancour and said, 'How did you decide it was me?'

'Partly by elimination. We knew that Debbie had been involved with an older man: there were various possibilities, but you always seemed the likeliest. The place where the body was disposed of suggested knowledge of the locality; as the place is nowhere near any public footpath, a member of the golf club was the likeliest of all to think of such a place to lose a corpse.'

Minton considered these things, then nodded a reluctant acceptance. He said with an air of modest pride in his cunning, 'I never gave my name when I tried to arrange the abortion.'

'No. But you wrote the number down for Debbie. We found it in her room. It was easy enough to compare the figures with samples on other material we took from this house. Figures are almost as individual as handwriting, you know, in the hands of an expert.'

Minton nodded; he had the air of a man who had discovered a minor piece of useful knowledge, which could be stored away for future use. Then he appeared to dismiss the matter of his guilt as being now satisfactorily established. He said resentfully, 'That vicar had a thing going with Debbie for a while.'

'The Reverend Jackson? He did indeed, though I doubt if Debbie was ever very disturbed by it. But he's a weak man, Derek, and you should have thought of that. Weak men are more dangerous to you than strong men, when you have things to hide.'

'He told you?' Suddenly, he was outraged. Then the annoyance dropped away from the thin face, and puzzlement stole in to replace it. 'But he couldn't have done. He doesn't even know who killed Debbie.'

'Nevertheless, he told us, Derek. Indirectly, of course. He told us how you'd been to see him, and why. How you wanted to know just what she'd said to him on that last night. That was significant to us, if not to the Reverend Joseph Jackson.'

'I had to know if she'd mentioned my name to him as a lover. But she hadn't. He didn't even suspect me; he was just terrified about what he'd done himself: he thought I was going to beat him up for that.' Minton allowed himself a little grin at the recollection of the clergyman's terror and his own success in deceiving him. It was the first hint of a psychopathic vanity.

'No. She merely told him about an older man and asked for advice. What would you have done if Jackson had known about you? Killed him?'

Minton considered the proposition as calmly as if it had been the purchase of a new set of golf clubs. There was an absence of moral awareness about him which was quite chilling. 'Perhaps I would have killed him. He'd abused Debbie, you know – there would have been quite a lot of sympathy for me. Perhaps I could have convinced you that he'd killed Debbie.' He smiled at each of them in turn, challenging them to deny it.

Peach said sharply, 'You'd never have got away with that, Derek.' He was the more vehement because he was not at all sure that he was right. Tommy Tucker for one might have seized upon the neat solution such an event would have offered.

They took him out to the police car then, once they had radioed in to the station. A neighbour greeted Derek Minton uncuriously over the garden fence as they went, and the murderer replied as cheerfully as if he had been going out with friends. Lucy Blake wondered if he realized at that moment that he would never walk up that path again.

She thought as they drove through the streets that she should feel triumphant. Perhaps that would come later. Perhaps she and Percy would go out and celebrate. For the moment, she could think only of that photograph of a pretty, carefree girl on the window-sill of the lounge they had left.

And of the woman who would return to contemplate it in an empty house.